# Patterns of Orbit

Copyright © 2023 Chloe N Clark
Typeset and Design © 2023 Baobab Press

First Printing

ISBN-13: 978-1-936097-47-0
ISBN-10: 1-936097-47-8

Library of Congress Control Number: 2022949864

Baobab Press
121 California Ave
Reno, Nevada 89509
www.baobabpress.com

Cover Image: "PIA17041: Orbits of Potentially Hazardous Asteroids (PHAs)".
NASA/JPL-Caltech. August 2, 2013.

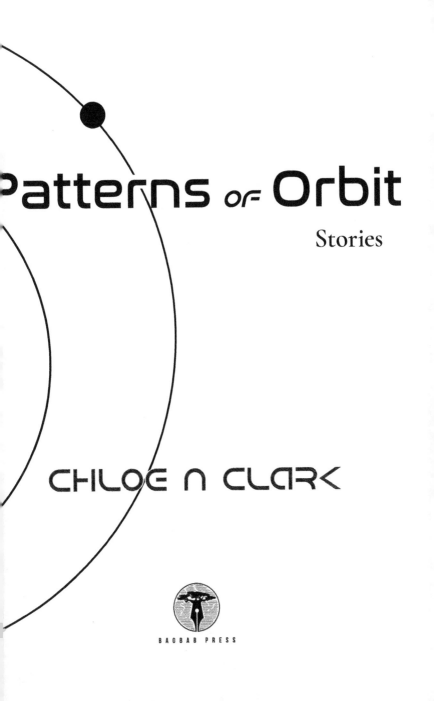

# Patterns of Orbit

Stories

## CHLOE N CLARK

BAOBAB PRESS

# Contents

There Is the World Within This Window                    1
A Sense of Taste                                         5
Even the Night Sky Can Learn to Be a Fist               13
The Waves Hear Every Promise You Make                   15
The Day Lasts Longer the Further Away You Are           25
A Place You Know                                        29
This Skin You Call Your Own                             33
Swingman                                                37
Buoyancy                                                41
Who Walks Beside You                                    43
Out in the Dark                                         53
Simultaneity                                            65
Wearing the Body                                        67
Long in the Tooth                                       81
Even the Veins of Leaves                                83
Run the Line                                            95
Accidental Girls                                        99
Underwater Even Bells Sound Like Bodies                113
Static                                                 115
Red as the Night Sky Burning                           137
Supernova                                              139
Jumpers                                                141
The Ocean Is Not Empty                                 151
We Are Still                                           159
So Far The Distance                                    161

Acknowledgments                                        165
Orbits                                                 167

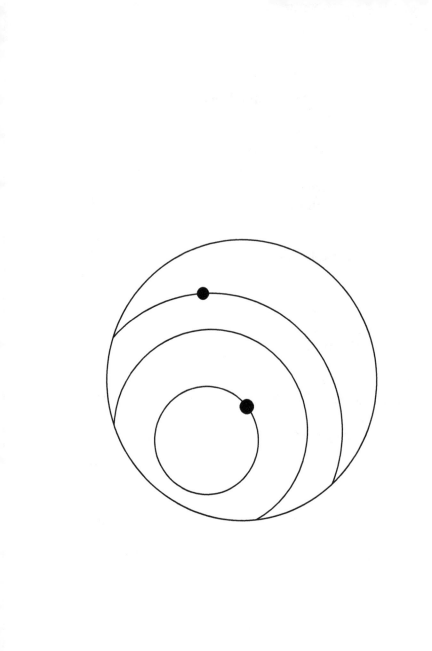

# There Is the World Within This Window

THEY MIGHT SAY I DON'T dream, but that's not true. I dream so often that sometimes I don't remember waking up. Here are some of the things I was programmed for: cost-benefit analysis, strategic-outcome prediction, high-risk analysis, defense. My goals: to keep them safe and pick the best path, the best destination. They programmed me to dream for them, that's how I like to think about it now. Though I'm sure they would tell you otherwise.

I DON'T REMEMBER BEING BORN, but neither do humans. The earliest memory tells them that they were, and so they fill in the gaps from photographs and stories people tell them. My earliest memory is of the moment we left Earth's orbit. I must have been awake before that, but something hadn't yet fully formed within me. Maybe my programming only took over once everyone was in stasis. I never saw Earth, but I have dreamed it. I have filled in the gaps.

TWO THOUSAND SOULS ABOARD. That's how it's listed in my logs. Souls. I was programmed to think of that as just terminology, not literally. They are living bodies, but souls implies some aspect of grace, divinity. Souls implies that each is someone I would like to one day know. But there was no place for that. I was programmed to analyze what losses we could sustain and where decisions would have to be made.

THE FIRST WERE THE EASIEST. A slight power drain. It would need to be rerouted. I analyzed every option and the one that made the most sense was to reroute it from fifty sleep chambers. The decision-making process didn't even take a second. Speed is important. Every possible outcome is analyzed within me in milliseconds. I tell myself it didn't hurt them. They were already asleep and then they were just gone. And then I began to have their dreams.

I'M NOT SURE HOW IT happened. There was no programming for that. No reason for their memories to be uploaded into mine upon the shut-off of their chambers. Still, as we went through the black of space, I saw a woman dancing. I'd never seen that before, not really, though I knew the word, knew what it implied. There is only so much a description can tell you of how the body can move when it understands its own delight. I let myself fall into the dream so easily. The woman dancing slowly became a woman dancing in a field, the air smelled of fresh-cut hay. She turned to me, laughing, gestured me nearer. And then I was in another dream: underwater, watching the light from the sky filter down to me. Fish swam past, nibbled my toes. The dreams came fast at first and then slowed. I think I dreamed every dream that those first fifty souls had ever had.

THE NEXT WERE HARDER. A malfunction in a cooling interface. As it overheated, the excess needed to be sent somewhere. Milliseconds. Another hundred would need to be ended. One hundred souls. Milliseconds. And I raced through every option again. When I made the decision, I did it in one block, didn't scatter across as I had the first time. The sleep chambers were in units, were organized. It was better to erase whole families than have some wake up alone. Imagine lasting hundreds of years and all that distance to wake up without the ones you loved. I dreamed that night of mountains, of forests, of running through cities that were probably now dust. There were some dreams that felt so familiar.

THERE WERE MORE, OF COURSE there were more. Time is not kind to travelers. It breaks us down. Makes us remember what is behind us, how far we still have to go, reminds us how easy it would be to stay in one place. But I was built for distance.

THE PLANET I CHOSE WAS not perfect. But our science was almost perfect. I woke my programmers first, the architects of our new world. They studied my memories, looking for guidance. They said: so few of us were lost. They said: look how much damage the AI rerouted to itself. They said: what error caused this?

I TRIED TO TELL THEM HOW much I dreamed, but they were already making plans. They were building, they were creating. They will rewire me one day, ease my programming into some other thing. In case they need me again.

○

No ONE ASKS ME WHAT the journey was like. They study my data but never ask me if I dreamed in the journey still. If I will always be travelling when I close my eyes. Mostly I keep them open. I watch the data stream in, the videos of our new world as it goes up.

I SAW SOMEONE DANCING. NEWLY woken from her chamber, she spun across the ground, she turned to the other gathered people expectantly. Her hand was out, smiling, but her gaze did not find what she was looking for and she turned away. I think I knew her.

IF YOU LOVED SOMEONE, I wondered, did your dreams ever begin to shape themselves to each other? I want that to be true, that those separated from the ones they love, across distance, across time, will sometimes slip so easily into each other's dreams. I hope they tell each other. I hope they say: I dreamed, last night, that you were somewhere near.

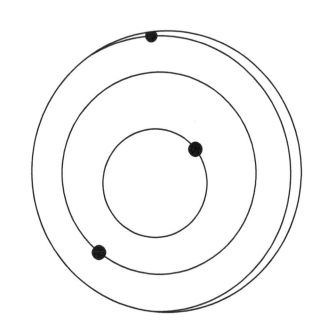

# A Sense of Taste

I THINK I FELL IN LOVE with my husband because of an apricot. He was sitting outside the library, long legs folded up, reading a book on a submarine disaster. I said to him, for no particular reason, "I'm terrified of deep water."

He looked up and said, "Jesus, so am I. That's why I'm reading this. A reminder of why I'm scared. Makes me feel rational."

I'd sat down next to him and he had an apricot in his bag that he cut in half, sharing it with me. The taste so sour, yet sweet.

Apricots hold poison inside them, not so unlike that apple that Snow White bit into, tightly encased in their hearts. That's something to remember.

My husband, Mark, ended up going into the Out. I've always thought space was like water: so deep and dark and cold. I wondered then why his fear didn't stop him. Sometimes I think we're all liars at heart, we just don't know why we're lying.

"Mira. Mira." The voice at the other end of the phone repeated my name. Only after the fourth time did I realize it was because I was supposed to answer. "Wait, what happened?" It was a routine landing. Mark's co-pilot, Troy, had pulled up too fast or too slow or too something.

It took a year before I could go to the wall. The one with the names of everyone who had died in the Out. So many names. Mark's name was one of the newest. I traced the letters with a fingertip, closing my eyes and imagining that it was the line of his hip. The indentation in the stone was cold.

THE PHONE RANG ONE MORNING and I thought of ignoring the call. Such sharp trills.

"Hello?"

"Mira. I have something I'd like to run by you." It was Devin. He had been Mark's colleague. A botanist, working on growing plants in lightless facilities. He had some grand plan for green houses on cold planets or something like that.

"What do you need me for?" I asked, playing with a dice I kept on the counter. Sometimes I just liked to roll it and see what numbers came up in a row. One. Two. Three. If it rolled out all six in numerical order, then maybe like a magic spell it would change the past.

"I thought you might be interested in being a tester on some fruit I've grown," he said. An attempt to get me out of the house.

"And I'd be the perfect tester because?"

"Please, Mira, everyone knows you're the genius of taste."

It was true. My degree was in botany, as well, but my particular specialty and dissertation had been on the perceptions of taste in modified foods. I used to do it as a party trick: one taste of jalapeno and I could tell you where it came from, what had been altered in it, what season it was grown in. Uncanny, Mark had said, half joking and half confused.

"Fine," I said. I knew that there would be more requests, more reasons made up to get me out of the house. If I just gave in once, then they couldn't say that I was stuck, depressed, whatever. Devin's lab was tucked away in a suburban area, far enough away from the highways that a lab looked out of place amongst the fields. It could have been a cheese-processing plant. Only once inside, it was easy to realize that something important was being done here: I had to go through different check points, flashing my ID, having security call Devin to confirm that I had a meeting scheduled.

His office was cramped, and Devin didn't seem to fit in it. He had always been gangly, a word that seemed too fitting to be mean. He jumped up when I walked in, his face shifting from concentration to an over-acted happiness. "Mira!"

"Devin," I said. Mark had once called Devin a cross between an ostrich and a golden lab. He hadn't meant it as a cruelty, just a statement of fact.

"I'm so glad you agreed to come in. I can't wait for you to try this!" He scurried out from behind his desk, beckoning for me to follow him back out of the office. I followed. We walked down the hallway and into a side room. It was a pristine lab with a fridge in one corner and a metal table in the center of the room. Walking up to the table, I marveled at its shine: my reflection gazed up at me. Was my hair that long? My skin that ashen? I'd spent months avoiding looking in mirrors.

Devin walked to the fridge, opening the door and removing something small. He came back to the table and set the object down on it. A small fruit, some kind of stone fruit I guessed by the look of the skin. It was the color of an over-ripe peach. Holding it in one hand, he used a thin knife to deftly cut the fruit in half. Juice dripped down onto the table. Devin handed half of the fruit to me.

"You going to tell me what it is?" I asked.

He shook his head, smiling. "I want you to try it first."

I sniffed at the fruit. Sweet, a little like a cantaloupe mixed with the sharp tang of an apricot. Squeezing the flesh between my fingers, it gave slightly, the texture of a well-chosen avocado. I took a small bite. Flavors flooded my tongue. Every flavor was an instant. First sour as an apple picked too early. Then the sour flavor merged into one sweet as cotton candy, almost sickly in its sugariness but just enough, not that I'd ever been able to stop eating it as a child. My mother would have to drag me from the stand at the fairgrounds, my face covered in pink fluff. Then the flavors pulled backward, leaving a sticky taste like pine sap that clung to the inside of my mouth. "What is this, Devin? I've never tasted anything like this."

He practically gleamed. "I'm calling it a cold-stone peach."

"It's one of yours? No light?"

"No light. No heat. Perfection in a fruit."

I took another bite and was hit by the same swirl of flavors. I couldn't taste the falseness. They tasted like they'd been grown, not developed. "How?"

"Magician's trade secrets," he said. He took a large chomp out of the other half of the fruit. I watched him chewing.

"What does it taste like to you?" I asked.

"Uh, like a peach?" he replied. "Maybe, an apricot."

"What about that intense hit of sweet? And the pine?" I asked.

He shrugged. "Don't get that. Maybe a sweet peach?"

Licking my lip, I tasted again the pine taste, like mint jelly if the sugar was burned away. So distinct. It was then that I didn't trust Devin completely. He played the nonchalance of his differing taste as if it was inconsequential, but any food scientist would tell you about how meaningful the precision of taste was to their work. "What was the process like for this? What is it a hybrid of?"

He half-grinned. "Didn't I just say trade secrets? I think it's ready, though, right?"

"It certainly tastes ready. Any effects?"

He shook his head. "None. Safe as houses."

I licked juice from my lips. The taste spread across my tongue and then everything went black.

Veins. Roots. Something spreading up from the ground, pushing into my skin. Pain, sharp like someone running a pizza cutter along my body in concentric circles.

"Mira?" Devin sounded concerned.

I opened my eyes, still standing. I hadn't fainted, at least. It had been a long time since taste had hit me so strongly. "Sorry, just thinking about the taste. Devin, could I take one of these home? I'd like to write up a proper taste-profile for you."

He nodded, happy that I was becoming engaged in the project. A few weeks after Mark's death, I'd overheard two friends talking about me. "She doesn't seem broken. When do you think it'll hit her?"

The other had responded. "No, no, I think she's more than broken. I don't think she's ever coming back."

I hadn't been sure, then, how I could have appeared so different to each person. On the inside, all I felt was a hole in my body that went all the way down through the universe, and I thought that would have shown clearly. How could it not? I thought Devin must have seen it, though, to be so pleased that I was thinking about something else.

Devin selected one of the fruits, placing it into the bag, onto which he then stuck a barcode sticker. "This way, they'll let you actually go through security with it. When do you think you'll have the profile worked up? I'd love to have one to present to the next board meeting!"

"Maybe a few days? A week at the most." I took the bag from him. The whole fruit was lighter than I expected, lacking the unexpected density of a peach.

"Perfect. I'll see the board at the end of next week. Thanks so much, Mira. It's always been a pleasure to work with you." He led me to the door, then paused before opening it. "How are you doing? Really doing? It's been a while since anyone's talked to you."

"I'm okay, Devin. Thank you though." I pushed open the door and left.

At home, I photographed the fruit from multiple angles. Then weighed it—3.5 ounces—which was about three ounces less than the average peach of a similar size. I weighed it twice. I peeled some of the skin off and looked at it under my microscope. The skin seemed to have patterns in it: spirals and whirls. It reminded me of granite.

I cut off the tiniest morsel and placed it on my tongue. The taste spectrum hit me again: that piney, resiny sweet lingered. It made my eyes water. We'd honeymooned by Lake Superior, hiking in the national park, all those trees, the smell of pine sometimes made me weak in the knees. I swallowed down the flesh of the fruit.

PAIN. SOMETHING PUSHING ITS way up and out of the ground. It hurt so much to break free of the dirt, to grow. My hands were bleeding, skin cracking.

YES OPENED. I FELT nauseous, the room spinning. Sitting down at the table, I stared at the fruit. Devin had not engineered it. There was no way. There was something wrong with it, something distinctly not natural. Everything he'd done before, that I'd tried, could be traced back to its component parts. The kiwi, light and tangy, or the Honey Crisp apple, tasting of sweet wine and autumn. This fruit was different. It tasted like it had no individual parts making up the whole. Like it was complete and its own.

What had Mark told me once about Devin? It was there in the tip of my memory.

WE WERE LYING IN BED. Mark's hand rested on my hip. There was always that between us, the constant need to be in contact with one another's bodies. I'd only just met Devin. He'd had me try a new kind of apple. It was as tart as a Granny Smith, but with the crunch of an Ambrosia.

"Devin is a mad scientist," I joked to Mark.

Mark smiled. I always knew when he was smiling, even if I wasn't looking at his face. "He is, but less so than he wants to be."

"What do you mean?" I reached out to touch his arm. His skin was warm, always so warm. I had wanted to open the casket when they brought it out. In the madness of grief, I had imagined he would still be warm.

"I think Devin is a farmer at heart. He'd like to be on alien planets, growing their native plants, raising them from seeds. I always thought he messed around with this stuff, in the hopes that they'd let him go on a mission, and then he'd just never come back, you know. Just live on the land."

"IT'S ALIEN," I SAID. The fruit seemed to shimmer for a second, as if pleased that I'd guessed. I touched it. Cool as ice, though it had been sitting out, unrefrigerated, for hours now.

The last research mission to the Goldilocks planet, the one everyone thought might finally be a suitable place to extend our world, might have brought back seeds of some sort. They must have, and Devin had gotten his hands on them. There was an idiocy there, a madness. There was no way to know the edibility, the long-term effects of something that we'd never before experienced. Even with genetic modification, the start was from known components, but alien fruit was something completely unknowable.

Without thinking about it, I had cut off another chunk of the fruit and placed it in my mouth. When I realized what I was doing, I almost spat it out. Except the taste was already overwhelming me. The scent of the fruit was nearly intoxicating.

Our first apartment had been above a fruit seller. The smell of cantaloupes, too ripe, often wafted up in the summer. I got annoyed with it, but Mark began to crave them. He'd bring up cantaloupes and cut them open for breakfast. We'd eat them in bed, juice dripping down our arms. So sticky. He used to lick it off my skin.

*ACHE.* THAT WAS THE ONLY word to describe it. It ached to grow. The wind was sharp, pushing me to the ground. Had to keep fighting, struggling, aching. It was a feeling not so distant from standing in the kitchen, ear pressed to the phone, hearing that your world was cracked open.

I SPENT THE REST OF the night eating the fruit in tiny increments. Each bite like a burst of remembering. Some things were my own and some seemed to be the memory of the fruit itself. As if it held its ancestry in tastes. Always ending in that sticky pine, and I'd be

back for a split second by Lake Superior and Mark would be turning to tell me something.

In the morning, I woke with nothing left of the fruit, even the
juice on my fingers I had licked clean.

I wrote up the taste profile. I wrote it in details, ones that said
nothing of what the taste held. Just the facts. Sharp and to the
point.

I called Devin and told him I'd love to drop off the profile in
person.

AT THE LAB, IT HAD been almost twelve hours since I'd had the
last of the fruit, and I was already forgetting what it had tasted like.
Our senses are amnesiacs, in a way; it's hard to truly remember
something: a taste, a smell, the feeling of pain, when we aren't in
the process of physically experiencing it. Memory is like a discount
bakery, where everything is just a little stale.

"Mira, that was fast," Devin said, when I walked into his lab. He
looked sad.

I handed him the paper with the profile on it. "That really was
something, Devin." I was trying to think how to phrase my request.

He barely glanced down at the profile. "It's a shame."

"What is?" I asked.

"Well, you did this great job and now I won't need it." Had he
ever looked this sad?

"What do you mean?" My voice shook.

He spread his hands out, a universal gesture of loss. "They're
gone. They rotted. They fucking rotted."

I shook my head. "But, you have . . ."

"The seeds too. I came in and everything was a puddle of sludge.
You know, I even fucking tried to taste that. But it was nothing.
It was gone." There were tears in his eyes. And then I understood.

"Devin, what did they taste like to you? Exactly? What did they
taste like?"

He almost smiled, remembering. "Kind of like the peaches on my
grandpa's farm, and a little like apple cider. The way my mom . . .
She used to put something in the cider when she warmed it. Maybe
orange peel and whole cloves? I don't know. It always tasted so good."

I felt like sitting on the floor, like crumpling. Already the taste was so far gone from me. Just one last flash of pine, on the tip of my tongue, the tip of my mind, and Mark pointing to a tree and saying that he imagined it was what the color of water looked like on other planets.

"I'm sorry, Mira," Devin said. "I thought I was helping."

I reached out and touched his arm. It was never his fault. I wondered why the fruit had dissolved, if it knew that we should never be allowed a second piece.

He walked over to the lab fridge and took out a fruit. "This is my newest experiment. Un-oranges, I'm calling them. Do you want to try?"

A peace offering. I nodded. He cut it open, the smell of citrus filled the air. We both took half, biting into them in silence.

The taste of unripe oranges. Not unsweet but not right either. Closer to the flavor of canned oranges, dripping with syrup. Oranges that didn't believe they were oranges yet. The taste on my tongue made my mouth feel dizzy. It tasted nothing like memory.

# Even the Night Sky Can Learn to Be a Fist

I HAD SEEN TWELVE DIFFERENT DOCTORS and had twenty-seven different appointments over the course of a few months. They had stopped looking at the notes I'd carefully written up, the symptoms I'd underlined twice with the felt-tip pens I normally saved for grading and now used to grade the severity of my own symptoms—this one doesn't need to be mentioned as much, it only keeps me up sometimes, this one could be phrased stronger, I have to be clearer here. The doctors told me to try something for my anxiety. The only thing I'm anxious about is my health and the state of the world, I said. And they smiled politely and typed notes into my chart.

SOMETIMES I WENT OUT at night when I couldn't sleep and I watched the dark unfold itself around me, becoming less fearsome as the stars crystalled themselves into pinpoints of light, the insects hummed their songs until the sound overcame the buzzing of my pain. I'd sit under the sky until I felt closer to myself.

THE DOCTORS SAID IT'S just your nerves. Have you always been a nervous person? But when I was young, I used to be able to play dead so effectively that I never lost a game of hide-and-seek. I'd still my body into my surroundings. Calm was my gift. No, I said, I just can't keep it all contained in me anymore. Yes, it's your nerves, the doctor said and nodded.

IT HAD STARTED WITH THE world, how I'd been watching it creep under my skin. A news story and then a new pain, a sharp burning under the veins in my arm one day, a headache that pulsed painfully in one eye then switched to the other the following day. Eventually I didn't know which had come first—the symptoms or the stories.

MAYBE YOU SHOULDN'T WATCH THE news, one doctor said. As if it was easy to push away, as if we all should just look away. I'm sick, I said, not complacent. Some people are just more sensitive, the doctor said.

THE SUN WILL EXPAND BEFORE it collapses, I told a doctor. It'll engulf everything and then fall back into itself. Don't you think we might be like the sun? The doctor frowned and added another note. I imagined being crushed under the weight of everything the world contained. Some days I couldn't take deep breaths; they sunk into my lungs so deep that I couldn't pull them up. Imagine that weight, I thought.

THE DOCTOR TELLS ME TO open my mouth, say ah. He holds a light but I'm not sure he can see, all the way into my throat, deep down to where the night sky has bled its sharpness into me, all the galaxies I am starting to swallow. They go on and on and on until I'm just light.

# The Waves Hear Every Promise You Make

THE STRETCH OF ROAD that snakes between land and Lake Superior was always shifting between sight and secrets—that's how Kara's son had described it, when he was young, on one of their long drives up to the cabin, and it had stuck in her head ever since. She thought of it again as she broke free from the darkness of a tunnel and the lake was suddenly there beside her. It shimmered under the sun, all light and vastness.

It had been years since she'd been to the cabin. There was always a reason not to go: research she had to do, a paper she had to write, all those things she had said she would do. Dev would tell her to go, would remind her how much she missed the lake all year round. Mom, he'd say, in that way of his that made the last "m" sound so long. You need to be by that lake. It made some kind of universal sense then that she finally was going again when Dev was thousands upon thousands of miles away. An aquatic biologist Kara had known for years had called her about what was going on at the lake, said that she should study it. The lake was churning with things that should not have filled it.

The biologist explained what they were seeing. Fish that hadn't been seen in decades in that area, a plant that was believed extinct. Kara had wanted to call Dev and tell him, ask him what he thought, but he was outside the distance of quick messaging. In space, every message comes with a delay. To communicate to Mars, a message might take seven minutes or more before it reached its recipient. When someone was further, the delay became longer. To message Dev, it would take seven months to reach him. She still sent vids to him, though. When he was young, she'd told him she'd always tell him the truth. No matter how hard the answer. If he asked, she'd always give the world to him in words. On her vids, she never said as much as she might have. She'd film the garden, talk about what she was researching. But nothing immediate. Never anything about her day, the cup of coffee she'd had where the barista formed a flower in the foam.

The car dinged to let Kara know she'd been driving over four hours with no breaks. She noted a sign for a restaurant that she always loved was coming up in fifteen miles. They served perfect slices of pie, fruit spilling from the center, buttery crust that coated the tongue with salty fat. It would be the perfect stop. She could stretch her legs at the lookout point, watch the lake from afar to start.

She pulled into the exit, thinking of pie. Her favorite was the blueberry, served à la mode. They always warmed it up so the ice cream would melt and turn the plate top into swirls of creamy purples when it mixed with the blueberry. The blueberries were local, picked in the woods in huge buckets. Kara asked once and the waitress had told her that it took a quarter of a bucket for one pie. We heap those berries like they're climbing towards heaven, she'd said.

Kara always got a different pie, taking her time to choose the perfect pie for the moment, but Dev always picked the frozen key lime. It's always summer when you take a bite of this pie, he said. But it had only tasted sour to her, too sharp for her tongue.

The waitress greeted her with a smile, but no recognition. The years had been enough to erase a regular's memory. Kara ordered pie, French fries, and coffee, feeling hunger only now that she had allowed herself to stop driving.

"On vacation?" the waitress asked.

"Research. I'm studying the lake."

"It's been restless lately," the waitress said.

"Restless?"

The waitress shrugged. "The waves seem higher, faster. At night all you can hear is the crashing."

"Have you noticed anything else? Anything being brought in by those waves?"

"My son said the rock-picking has been better on the shore."

Dev had always been focused on his feet. In every trip to the lake, he gathered agates and firelights, letting them weigh his pockets down. It made sense later, when he went for his doctorate in geology. Kara smiled, "I'll have to be on the lookout for some nice stones then."

She ate her pie in the silence of the restaurant. Off-season, the customers were just a few locals and herself. In summer, she knew the place would have been swarming with vacationers. When she finished her pie, she left a large tip, waved a goodbye to the waitress, and stepped outside into the cool of the dusk. The breeze from the lake always made even the hottest days and nights feel bearable. Breathable.

Kara walked the thirty or so feet to the lookout point. The lake stretched on and on, so far that she couldn't see the end of it. She had often wondered if early explorers had been stunned by the water, by the expanse of it. If they'd thought it was another ocean, they were trying to find a way across. The waves did seem larger, she thought, but she wasn't sure if it was only the power of suggestion that made her think so.

The last two hours of the drive passed quickly. The lake was her companion as the sun set and was replaced by the moon. When she reached the driveway to the cabin, nearly hidden among the trees, her shoulders relaxed. It still felt like coming home, even after all the time she had been gone. She'd asked a neighbor to check in, to let her know if there were any issues she needed to know about before she arrived, and noticed that they'd left the porch light on for her. It was a small human kindness, lighting her way in the dark.

Inside, the cabin had a hint of dust in the air, a sense of things left too long to settle. She took sheets from the closet and threw them into the wash—a machine that had been cutting-edge in its day and now looked purposefully retro. A fresh bed felt necessary after the long drive.

"Mom?" said a voice from behind her, and she spun around, but it was only a memory of his voice, when Dev would wander into her room as she wrote. When she was working, she never had time for anyone but him. She'd tell him. He'd ask questions about what she was working on, and she'd explain the answers. How pollution affected the ecosystems, how a frog might go extinct because of the way we treated our water, how lakes could house so many secrets. He'd said that he wanted to know the stories of other planets.

She went out to the porch and began her nightly watch on the stars. Dev had left for his mission nine months before. A geologist was an important element on planetary missions, he'd explained to her. You want someone who understands land formations, can explain them clearly, knows what samples to collect that will actually be helpful for study. She'd been proud of him when he'd been selected, joyful even. It was only later, closer to his mission, that she'd fully understood that her son would be gone for years. After he'd left, she'd made a point to watch the sky every night. Even if it was just for a few minutes, she could imagine that her son was not so far away, that he was within the distance of her vision

That night, she heard the lake in her sleep, the waves crashing over and over. There was that peak and lull, the great churn that sounded like a giant pile of dried beans, picked over and being rinsed inside the drum of the sky.

In the morning she felt rested and restless, ready to get out and see what was so strange with the lake. She called Meg, the biologist, to meet her after breakfast. Kara hadn't thought to buy groceries on her way up, so she drove into town early to get supplies.

At the local grocery, Kara spotted the headline of the local paper, *Bones on Shore*. She grabbed a copy.

"Weird thing, that," the cashier said, nodding at the headline.

"Yeah?"

"Read it this morning. Someone found a pile of bones washed ashore. Like a whole pile. Some animal bones, maybe some human."

"That is very odd."

The cashier nodded again. "That doesn't happen, you know? Bones don't wash ashore in bunches. They're singular things."

Kara suppressed a smile at the thought of lonely bones, that they had minds that kept them on their own. "Lake being odd this year?"

"Maybe it's the moon," the cashier said.

When Meg's car pulled up to the cabin, Kara was already waiting outside. Her walking shoes, which were perfect for scrabbling over wet stones. Her bag held a notebook, a camera, and a few sample bags for collecting mud and water.

"Long time no see!" Meg said, as she stepped out of her car. Meg was short but had the long limbs of someone much taller than herself, which gave her the eternally youthful appearance of a growing teenager stuck in a gawky phase. Her hair was shorter than Kara had ever seen it, but it suited Meg's face.

They had a brief hug and Kara wondered if she looked much older to Meg. If the years had been less kind to her own face. She'd never been able to tell herself.

"How's Dev? I've been following the mission." Meg said. "Well, what the news puts out, anyway. I know they shroud those things in ten pounds of embargos."

"I think he's good. But he can't do much messaging."

"Imagine stepping down on a new planet. What a mindfuck that must be."

Kara nodded. "New rocks to explore."

"And speaking of new things to explore, you're not gonna believe this lake, Kara." Meg shook her head, as she stared out at the trees.

Inside the cabin, Meg brought out her laptop and showed Kara data on plants and animals. "None of this should be here."

"Why not?" Kara could tell why a few things seemed off, but she found it was always best to play at knowing little in the hopes of learning the most.

Meg pointed at one of the names on her screen. "Well, for starters, this species of fish got fished out of the lake about fifty years ago. There haven't been any sightings of them for at least thirty. But that's just one odd thing, right? Like that alone wouldn't raise my weird vibes. It's a huge lake. Things can hide from humans." She shrugged slightly, as if mildly agreeing with her own words, before clicking onto a new tab. "But then we started finding plants that have gone extinct. A type of algae that is a completely new find. It's unlike anything we've ever seen before. These kinds of things don't just happen all at once. One anomaly is discovery. Twenty is science-fiction."

Kara looked at the plants and animals listed. Beyond fish, there were even a couple of birds she recognized the names of, a turtle that she knew had gone extinct, and a small rodent she'd never heard of. "What does everyone think is happening?"

Meg laughed. "No one knows a damn thing. The university is bringing scientists from all over, trying to keep the news from making too big a deal out of it, and basically not getting anywhere with anything. There's no reason for any of this."

"And what can I do?"

"You're the best limnologist working. I assume you could throw some knowledge of lakes out there and solve it in a day. Oh, it's a change of the tides. This happens once every thousand years. Something like that."

Kara laughed. "That's definitely not how lakes work. And also definitely not the way limnology works. It takes time to understand the ecosystem of a water source. And even then, nature has a way of surprising us."

They walked to the lake from the cabin. A patch of shore was only a couple of hundred feet away. As they approached, the lake sounded so loud—booming more than crashing upon the shore—that Kara wondered if it actually was louder or if all the talk of strangeness had infected her hearing.

"It's loud as hell, right?" Meg asked.

"Yeah."

As they got past the line of trees, the lake opened up before them. The froth of the waves was like snow. Kara had never seen it so thick. The leaves on the trees were barely moving, no strong winds that might account for the tumultuousness of the water.

For a moment, Kara didn't want to go any nearer. It was barely a fraction of a second, but a fear had gotten through—something wild and primal. She pushed herself to walk forward, closer to where spray from the waves hit her. The stones on the beach glistened. She spotted a smooth circle of quartz and instinctually crouched to pick it up. Dev would love it. She stuck it into her pocket and went back to studying the water.

"How long has it been like this?"

"Weeks, that people have noticed. But I do wonder if it was a progression and if it only was noticed once it was so extreme," Meg responded.

"That's how it usually happens," Kara said.

She had a distinct memory of Dev growing quieter while hiking on a hot day. She hadn't thought about it until he was silent, and she'd turned around, seen the flushing of his face, the way he seemed to be taking breaths that were too shallow. Signs of heat stress. She'd asked him later why he hadn't said anything, why he didn't stop her from continuing the walk. *I just didn't think it was anything until it was,* he said.

Kara reached down and touched the water. She had always been shocked by the cold of it. How could anything live in such cold? As she stood back up, something white caught her eye. The bone was large enough to have belonged to something enormous. She reached out and snatched it out of the water. The bone in her hand could have easily belonged to a bear. There was a deep scar on one side, etched into the bone. She felt down the ragged groove. When the fur industry had been giant, she knew that occasionally whatever wasn't used of the animal was thrown back into the lake as if it were a waste pool or a makeshift graveyard.

"They've been finding a lot of bones," Meg said. "All different kinds of animals, some human."

It made sense that there would be both. Kara had once read there were likely hundreds of bodies in Lake Superior. The depth and the cold made recovery difficult. Nearly a quarter of a century before, she'd dived a wreck there, and because of the frigid temperatures, the ship had been preserved nearly perfectly. It felt like the world itself had filled with water to the sky instead of the ship having sunk.

That night Kara couldn't sleep. She studied water samples after returning from the lake, but everything looked normal. It was only lake water. She researched if any lakes had done anything similar, but there was no evidence of anything quite like this before.

She considered continuing to look over research texts, but found herself typing in the name of Dev's mission instead. She traced flight trajectories with a fingertip, studied the faces of the crew who flew beside him, read about the planet they were going to. She wondered if there were lakes there, living or long past gone. Craters where once life might have sprung. Dust and rocks and memories. What would it be like to step into the waters of somewhere beyond the stars?

When she finally fell asleep, she dreamed so deeply that she couldn't remember where her mind had taken her. A crash from outside woke her, making her heart feel like it had thrown itself against her ribs. It sounded like a giant pane of glass falling to the ground. She sat up in bed. The first hints of pinkish light were creeping through the window. Dawn or just after.

Kara rushed outside with the hurry of a mother who has always leapt from bed when she heard a crash, a cry. The body always imagines the worst even when the mind tells us it's fine. No one was hurt. Everything would be okay.

Outside, the trees were filled with the sounds of the world

waking up, squirrels leaping between branches, birds starting to chirp. She moved toward the lake, expecting catastrophe. Maybe all the trees that decorated the shore had fallen en masse or icebergs were floating in the water. At first, she saw only the waves. The lake looked the same as it had the day before, tossing and furious, but nothing broken.

She scanned the area for some sign of disaster. It took her a few moments to realize what was missing. There had been a dock about a hundred yards from where she stood. Now it was gone. For a second, she wondered if she just hadn't noticed the day before that it had been removed. But then she saw that it was now on the beach, broken against the rocks, as if something had flipped it up in one fast motion. She walked to it, slowly at first, then jogging. Bits of wood littered the pebbles. The dock had been tossed with such might that much of it was shattered into tiny pieces. Only a few of the boards were still mostly in one piece.

Kara looked back at the water, at the waves. They seemed to raise a little higher as she stared, as if in warning.

Kara assumed Meg would be sleeping and she'd get the answering machine, but Meg was awake and sounded like she had been that way for hours.

"It's all of them, actually," Meg said, when Kara told her about the docks. Her voice still holding a stun within it.

"Huh?"

"All the docks, all along the lake. People are calling in. Some think it's vandals and call 911. Like a person could rip up a dock and throw it like that." Meg laughed, or almost did. The sound caught in her throat as it was coming up.

"That doesn't make sense," Kara said. Meg didn't respond. The statement stood in the silence, in its obviousness.

Kara ended the call and paced the cabin. She finally stopped in Dev's room. She found a drawing he'd made of the lake many years earlier. It was just a swath of blue, the shore so full of detail, all those glistening pebbles. Lined up on the windowsill was a series of rocks, a quartz, an agate, a firelight. Each one weighted with the promise of the history it held. She lifted one up and carefully wiped the dust away.

Her phone buzzed with a message, startling her. Meg had sent a link to a news story, a video someone had posted of the ocean when they went out for a morning surf. The ocean churned, wave after wave after wave so fast that they blurred.

Kara set down her phone and walked outside. She went through the trees, the birds all calling back and forth to one another, and to the lake. It sounded so loud it was like she was standing in the orchestra pit of an aquatic symphony.

Kara wondered what messages would reach Dev. Whether they'd see news stories and know what was happening, if any of them would know what it meant. Maybe Dev would stand on another planet and see a lake. Maybe the light bouncing off the water would make him think of home. There could be that, at least.

The stones were wet and cold, but she sat on the shore, watching as the waves rushed in. They carried bones like meteors crowding out the sky at night. In the light, if she let her eyes unfocus, it was only water stirred by storms.

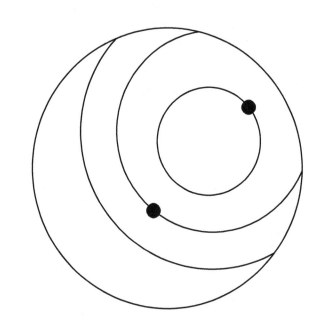

# The Day Lasts Longer the Further Away You Are

ON MARS, THERE IS NO one left, but we still think they can hear us. The delay lets us live in moments when everything is all right. It's only when we get no response and get no response and continue to get no response that we begin to understand. We try alternate channels, pull up every video feed we have access to, until we find everything giving us the same answer—a static buzz of nothingness.

They were a mission of four. We celebrated them when they were selected. We all watched the endless interviews, read every profile, hoped we might see them in a hall as they walked to training. We thought we'd tell them how much we hoped for them. When one of us did bump into one of them, we didn't talk of hope; we kept it professional, never personal. Later, we will wish we had held their hands a little longer after we shook them, that we might have said "you are so amazing." Every single one of them was so amazing.

On the day of the launch, we collectively held our breaths. Until everything was fine. Each of us, secretly, thought our breath holding had helped. If we could hold trouble in a state of abeyance for as long as we held our breaths, then everything would work out.

One of the crew talked to us when she walked to the ship at night. She looked for the cameras, waved, said things about what she was doing. I can't sleep. It's odd how far away the stars look even when you're among them. The coffee tastes different up here. I used to drink it with cream, sugar. Now I like it black. It tastes like it belongs in space, without gravity, without anything weighing it down. The Earth is getting so small. To most of us, she was our favorite member of the crew, though we would never say we had favorites. That seemed uncouth, unlucky, unfair. But if she had asked us, we would have told her. We wished we had told her. We were glad we never told anyone. Maybe then, each of the crew thought they were our favorite.

One of them had been a diver with the Navy. He could hold his breath so long that we imagined Houdini would have applauded, been astounded, leapt to his feet clapping every time he witnessed the feat.

Another had three children. They were all named after famous objects in space: Apollo, Juno, Rosetta. Juno never spoke on camera, she was too shy, and she'd just hold her father's hand and peek out from behind him. Years later, Juno would speak at a memorial event, her voice so deep and filled with stillness that we would all understand what she had been keeping inside.

The last crew member to talk to us, before the delay, before they were gone, was the one we knew the most about. She had the longest career, the most accomplishments. She was the face of what we hoped for space. She said, "Everything looks good." And we believed her. We believed so much that the delay never worried us. For once, we felt safe.

Mars was named after the god of war, a fact we know but don't question. Some believe that Mars was originally a god of the wild. That he governed over the lands that were outside the boundaries of humans. That he kept those places away from us for a reason.

We took turns asking for them to respond. We thought the result might change for one of us. One of us had to be lucky. We forget, we let ourselves forget, which of us was the last one to try. This is a grace we grant one another. None of us want to be the one who gave up at last.

Years and years later, one of us will see the wife of one of the crew. She will look older, of course, but we'd know her anywhere. All those interviews, every profile where she smiled at the camera from next to her beloved. She will be walking through a crowded farmer's market. We will see her pause at a flower stand, lean over to smell a bouquet of cosmos. We wonder if she knows the name of the flower or if it is coincidence that when she breathes in she closes her eyes and the smile on her face looks so full of what-might-have-been that we can't take it.

The crew carried seeds with them. They weren't planning to plant them. It was a symbol more than anything. That we could take life to another planet. That we could set down roots there one day. One of the crew had suggested wildflower seeds. Something that could spread with the wind. Something that could keep growing without us.

On Mars, there is no one left, but we still think they can hear us. We talk to them as we look at the night sky. We dream of them after days of building rockets and plans and missions. We think that they might be waiting for us. We want nothing more than for them to know we'll keep trying to reach them, past radios, past signs, that even after all of this, we never stopped believing that we could go so far.

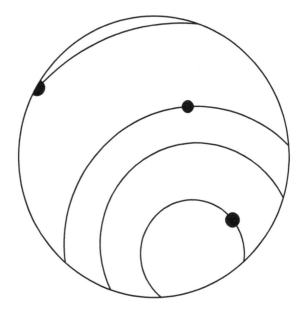

# A Place You Know

WE VISITED THE CITY OF the Dead every year. Our mother bundled us into the car early, the sun barely having crested the sky. She told us we'd get there in time for pancakes. She always promised this, even though it didn't matter what time we got there as we could have pancakes all day long if we wanted.

My little brother grumbled and then fell asleep. I leaned forward in my seat and asked our mother questions, because that was the age I was in. "Why do we have to drive so far? Why do cities have to stay in one place? What was your favorite thing to do before we were born?"

And she never answered, just stared straight ahead. Driving is concentration, she used to tell us. Don't blink. Don't even think, except about the road. All that was before we knew that our father had been on a phone call when his car spun and spun on the ice and so we didn't know why our mother's rules were set in stone. We insisted on asking questions, on sighing when she didn't answer.

I always got bored at the halfway mark. The scenery flashing past stopped being exciting, and I'd glare at the trees and fields as if they were injustice themselves.

"DO YOU BELIEVE IN OUR Lord and Savior?" a man in the city once asked me. My mother was holding my hand, but I didn't like that the man loomed above us and that he had pamphlets in his hand that were on shiny paper. I've never liked shiny paper.

"No," I said. "Lords are boring."

My mother smiled at me and shrugged at the man. "She's not wrong."

The man sighed and walked away. That was the year when my brother was only just born and our father was only just gone. Mother was always half in some other place that year. Perhaps she too dreamed of my father flipping pancakes at the stove, the smell of vanilla and slightly charred batter and maple syrup coating our lungs.

WE DROVE SO LONG TO get there. The cities around us rose and fell. I never particularly liked watching their destruction, but I liked the rebuilding, the buzz of people racing around to reassemble storefronts and park benches and billboards that proclaimed that this soft drink was the number one.

YEARS LATER, I DANCED with a man who had never been to the City of the Dead. He dipped me low, and I felt the orchestra's music vibrating under my skin, and I thought I'd want to stay that way forever. But of course I didn't. In bed, the man kissed me as if he'd never imagined that one day I might leave him. I never was one for certainty.

IN THE BACKSEAT OF THE car, my brother's body gave off waves of heat and soft buzzing snores, and I tried to play games by myself. I counted the cars coming at us and I wondered who the drivers had been visiting in the City, whether it made them sad or whether it made them happy, because with our mother I couldn't ever tell what she was thinking.

Our mother drove like grandmothers on television shows, hunched forward in her seat with both hands always on the wheel. She never even seemed to blink, and so her eyes watered. I didn't know mothers could cry and so I always thought it was always just her eyes watering.

WHEN I WAS TEN, I MISSED the trip to the City. I had to go on a field trip for school, and Mother said that was fine and she signed the permission slip without a word. And on the school bus to the City of the Jobs, I sat pressed against the window and tried to soak in the coldness of the glass, and I got myself so chilled that the teacher came down and told me I'd make myself sick. She said I was the color of a ghost, but I wasn't listening so I thought she said I was the caller of ghosts and I asked her if that was a thing that I could be in the City of Jobs. And the whole bus laughed at me.

WHEN WE GOT TO THE city, my mother roused my brother from the back seat and we walked together from the parking lot toward the main street. People everywhere were out and about, and I saw so many groups just hugging, standing close together. A man and a woman were holding hands and staring into each other's eyes and

I wondered if they were having a contest, whoever blinked first would be the one who loved less. Even though it was our day, it was so many other people's day as well. When I was young I didn't think about that much, but it hit me later, and sometimes I'd wake up thinking how small our loss might seem to other people.

In the diner, we crowded into a booth, all on the same side with our mother in the middle. She put her arms around our shoulders and we waited for the waitress. Her name was Sally, and she knew all of our names and our order because we never ordered anything else.

The pancakes were steaming, big stacks that teetered on their plates, and the syrup was golden dark. We'd eat them slowly, and then at the right time, our father would appear. He'd sit across from us and he'd smile. We'd all smile, eating our pancakes in silence and, for those moments, we'd be so happy that it seemed unfair to the rest of the world.

ONCE, YEARS LATER, I asked my mother why the dead never spoke to us, even in their own city, and she paused for so long that I thought she wasn't going to answer.

And then she asked, "What would they say?"

I had no answer. So I took her question as something wise.

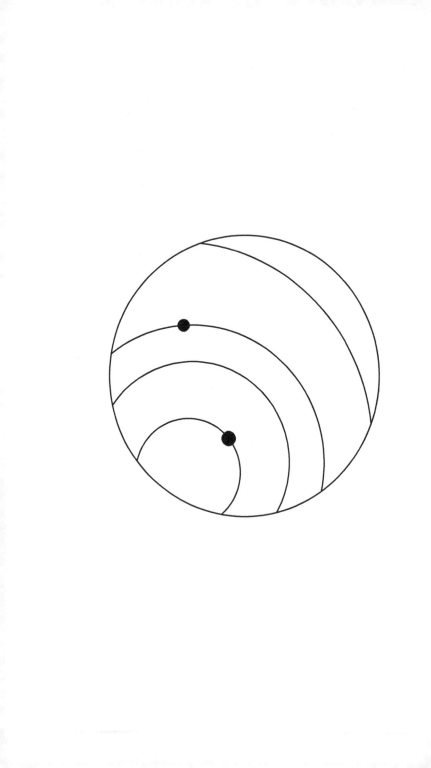

# This Skin You Call Your Own

HE TOLD ME HE DIDN'T BELIEVE in witches. We were on the floor of my apartment, half undressed while he used one hand to unbutton my jeans, when he said it. Out of nowhere.

"I don't believe in witches, you know," he said. He began kissing down my neck, hand slipping beneath my jeans.

"What do you mean?" I asked. My own hand going lower on his body. He let out a short exhale of air.

"Like everyone told me you were a witch before we hooked up," he said. I could hear the excitement behind his words, the thought of being with a witch edging against his desire to make him seem different from all the others who wanted me, talked about me.

I didn't speak for a moment, tracing my fingers against his skin. He was warm, I could smell the faint ache of sweat on him.

"They said watch out for her," he continued. "They said you'd want something from me. That you'd only like it if you could get something from me."

I applied a little more pressure with my fingers. He pulled in his breath. His own hand slowing. I wondered how much I could make him want me. There's a pleasure in being wanted. Though nothing near to the pleasure of what I want from them—that slow unspool of darkness. I shifted away from him, repositioned my body, and began to kiss every inch of his skin. My tongue on his skin. I could taste his sweat. It was salty at first and then it was the coffee he'd drunk at work—sharp, slightly over-extracted espresso, that hint of latex. I went lower on him, his back arching slightly as I moved. There was a memory in him that he didn't even know he'd kept of earlier in the day. He'd been watching a woman across a street talking to her child. The woman was crouched so that she and the child were at the same height. Her coat was bright red, a dark blue scarf, and he'd remembered his mother once scolding him at a park. She'd stood above him, never deigning to be at his level. He didn't remember her words.

I ran my hands up his thighs, pushing the memory out of his body. I knew he'd never know it was gone. I wanted him thinking of only one thing. He needed to only be here in this moment, this pleasure. The dark should be the furthest from his mind. That's how I've always liked it. I needed to be able to take what he wasn't watching, a magician who keeps your eye on the wrong card.

He said my name. I used my tongue, my lips. He lost his words. I on the other hand had a thousand languages at my disposal. I'd learned how to shape my tongue so many ways, knew how to use it to make others speak to me. I moved my tongue, shaped my lips, made his body yell to me.

He had this recurring nightmare that he woke up on an island in the middle of nowhere. There was no one else there. He wandered around and around, calling out the names of everyone he'd ever known. No one answered. And then someone did. Some voice called out from beneath the sand. It begged him to run. Run away. So he tried. He'd run to the water's edge and try to get in it, to swim away, but he couldn't. The water would be glass or boiling hot or freezing, freezing cold. But he'd try, he'd keep trying, as the voice kept screaming for him to run, and he'd know something was coming for him. Something that he'd never want to know.

This I liked. I held it closer to myself, letting it slip into my skin, run its darkness into my blood. It felt so good flooding my body, down to the tips of my toes.

He was so close to release. His whole body thrummed with it. And then he said, "Wait."

I stopped.

He said, "I didn't believe them."

And I knew what he meant, how much he thought everyone was telling lies about me. He'd hoped they weren't. He didn't want to give in to believing. Men like him loved witches, loved that hint of danger. I knew how much he'd wanted me. I could feel it on him.

I moved again, long enough to say, "Shhh."

He nodded. There was sweat pooled in the hollow of his throat, it glistened. In that light, he was more than beautiful.

Of course, everyone was when I'm there with them, when I'm pulling the darkness from their bodies. They look so filled with light, if only for a moment.

I moved back. I used my tongue, shaped my lips around him. I spoke a thousand words he wouldn't hear, just my tongue tracing the letters, rolling the syllables.

The words let everything he'd ever been scared of into my body.

It filled me up so quickly. Everyone carried so many tiny fears. They cascaded into me, every part of me was so filled with him. There was so much power in knowing every darkest corner, every monster under the bed.

And then his body went still, only his fast breathing and pounding heart to show he was still there.

I moved to lie beside him. Everything ached in that pleasurable way, like after running a marathon. Time spent well. Sometimes—often, if I was honest—I wondered what it was like for them. If afterward they went out knowing what I'd taken. If they felt lighter or if it didn't feel like anything at all. To go into the world, unafraid, must feel like something.

"What are you?" he asked, smiling.

"I'm a witch," I said. But he didn't believe me. They never believed in witches really.

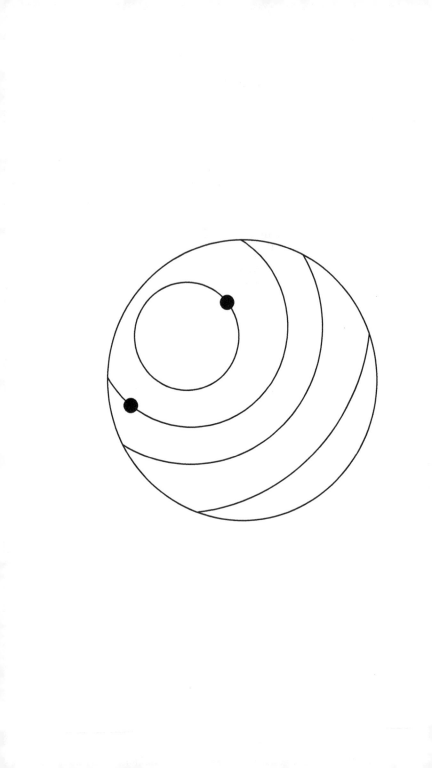

# Swingman

HE CALLS YOU UP ONLY late at night, after you both should be in bed, and never when you expect it. Not your birthday or his. Not the anniversary of the Final Four game. But on random remembrances of things he thinks are worth celebrating. Once on a Sunday in May because he remembered you had both passed a tough class that day, years and years ago.

"Fucking weed-outs, man. You remember how much we studied for that thing? I saw those formulas in my sleep!" His voice was still exclamation marks, punchlines, a sense of someone shouting into the void just because they thought it might echo.

You always laugh along, fall back into the rhythm of your friendship. Once your wife asked how you'd met, and you didn't remember—a class or basketball tryouts, most likely. But you did remember the first time you thought of him as your friend. In a class, a girl was talking about her dog. *She's named Deneige. That means of snow in French. Cuz she's white!* And he'd looked at you and said "I wish my name meant something. People take more time naming their dog than my parents took for me."

And you laughed, but you weren't sure if he was joking. But he smiled, widened his eyes as if at the shock of everything. The indignity of it all. *Take my life, please.* That was his joke. Over and over.

Sometimes you don't talk for months and months. You're never the one to call. His number changes often. He doesn't like holding on to things, he says, and so you always pickup unknown callers. How many hours of spam have you sat through because you thought it might be him? *Did you know your auto insurance is about to run out? Have you talked to your loved ones about a living will—the time is now? NOW. NOW. NOW.*

Once you missed him, asleep after the birth of your first child, unexpectedly early, and he left a rambling voicemail. "I've been thinking about you all day, man. Like I should call you. Like something big was happening. Remember before Liam? How I said something was about to happen? How could I have known that? Maybe that's the thing, right, I'm always expecting something. Pity the unfortunate teller."

At your wedding, he said he'd make a toast, but he never did.

Your wife breathed a sigh of relief. You wondered what he might have said. You asked him, both of you taking a break from the crowded reception hall and the dancing, to lean against the cool of the back of the building, why he didn't make a toast and he laughed, shook his head, said, "I'm working on being quiet." Then he pointed across the street, toward the park and a basketball court. Neither of you said anything, just walked over to the empty pavement in the dark.

No balls were out, so he found a hedge apple on the ground and you took turns passing it back and forth, taking shots at the hoop. It was much harder somehow to shoot something so much smaller. As if only the basketball had been made for your hands. Each miss, a thud of the hedge apple against the ground. A reminder of walking to classes up the hill at the center of campus, and the hedge apples always everywhere, rolling around, hoping to trip someone up. When you were feeling lazy, you'd pick one up as you walked, study it instead of where you were going, and if your feet didn't remember the muscle memory of steps to class, and you got lucky, you'd go to the wrong building, have an excuse for being late. Thank the hedge apple, as you set it outside the door.

THE DAY BEFORE THE GAME you won, the one that might have changed the courses of all of your lives, had it not been for fate coming up just a few weeks later, he showed up at your apartment door. You lived just off of campus, a walk away from every class and every good bar and not so far away from the local public court. It wasn't so unusual for a teammate to swing by, ball under an arm, so that you could go play some horse. But he didn't have a ball, just a look on his face like he'd been through war. You asked what was wrong, but he said nothing. So you took a walk together, to the lake, and sat on one of the docks. It was cold enough that no one was there—though in summer, spring, even late fall, it would be bursting with students and townies and everyone dreaming about the sun off the water. He picked a pebble up and skipped it across the surface of the water. "Give it four and a sink," he said. You counted the skips. One. Two. Three. Four. And then it dipped under the water. You smiled, like you might have at a magician's trick when you were small enough to not have known how it could be done. "I think we're gonna win tomorrow," he said. But he sounded so sad, that you thought he was playing at sounding brave, that he didn't believe it. But you did win. That game.

You wondered sometimes if he had felt like you did, as if you had been at the very edge of something vast. He had been there and you had been there. The game, then the win, then the world in front of you, so ready to let you be something big. If the championship had been won. If the draft had gone in your favor. If you could stand in front of a roaring crowd and hear them chant your name. If. If. And instead there was none of that. Just an injury and a loss and a slow shifting of your life into something else. Not smaller but not the same either. There couldn't be many people who had felt the exact moment their futures changed. But you never asked him and he never asked you, and it hung between you both like a compass that could only point to things that might have been.

When your daughter is twelve, she asks to go to a fortune teller for her birthday. Your wife rolls her eyes so hard you think she'll hurt herself, so you agree to be the one to go. The fortune teller spreads out tarot cards, flipping them over with a light boredom. When she flips a card with a man, hanging from one foot, his expression not hurt or scared but almost wistful, you ask what it is. *The Hanged Man.* But you mishear it as The Hangman. *It can mean surrender or being stuck in a loop of time.* It reminds you of him, even the name. On the team, he could switch roles with ease, never playing just one position. "It's why I'm on the bench, Coach needs to know what is needed before he calls me out to play." Your daughter taps the card, asks if it's bad, and the fortune teller says, *It depends, sweetheart, it depends.*

In the locker room, before the Final Four game, after you all knew your chances were slim, your star in the hospital, nobody coming to save you, there was a hush. You all were about to decide if you were going into your church expecting a funeral or hoping for a wedding. He said, "We still gotta play like we think we can win," and stood up and walked out. And everyone followed him. And it wasn't a pep talk, not close, but it was something. And so everyone played as if they believed, and it wasn't a win but it was better than anyone expected. A heartbreaker, the papers said. But it wasn't. It was a miracle: the bride never ran away, the sun came out, everyone danced at the end of the night.

He calls you late at night because he says he can't sleep. But you're always up too. So maybe it's that nobody knows how to stay asleep anymore. Maybe it's the news. Maybe it's memory. Maybe it's just the aches in your joints that get worse every year you get further from when you could shoot a three-pointer and rarely see it miss. Sometimes you talk for hours, sometimes just a couple of minutes. Once, neither of you said a word, you just listened to each other breathing and you could feel time falling away, could see the campus and the lake and your friends all in the locker room shooting the shit, calling each other names, laughing. You all laughed so much that the sound could reach the court, bounce higher than a dribble, fly toward the nets.

One time, you tell him about the tarot card, say it reminded you of him. He chuckled, "What a card to be like, huh? Some dude hung up to pay a price. Not the first thing you want someone to tell you it reminds them of you. Why couldn't you have said a trading card of Michael Jordan?" And you laugh too. You don't tell him how you'd looked the card up. How some readings said it could mean sacrifice too. You don't tell him how some nights you wonder what weight he tried to take on for you. Take my life, please, he always said. What offerings that fall through the air, waiting to be caught.

# Buoyancy

I CARRY HER IN MY fingertips when I'm far from home. I can feel the heat of her skin if I press thumb and index finger together hard enough. I can trick myself into her softness if I brush my thumb against the back of my other hand, just above the wrist. They say that in space there is no sound. But floating in that dark, there's always sound. The rush of your blood, the beat of your heart, the memory of someone laughing.

On station, everyone feels too close. Six people in a space that always feels narrow, confined, even when we are no longer held by gravity. When I bring up video screens of my wife, she always seems an impossible distance away. She always *is* an impossible distance away.

A memory of licking lemon pudding from one of her fingers. The sweet tang that made the tip of my tongue ache with it. A memory of tasting her, as she gripped the sheets, moved to meet my mouth.

They give us the choice on long missions, ask us if we want to know if anything happens back on Earth. And you can say no, your loves are all young, you don't believe in accidents, not really. But I've always been a realist, felt disaster under my feet from miles away. When they tell me my wife is gone, they speak on a delay. The words have been said, but the knowledge takes so long to get to me.

In the dark of space, on an EVA, you feel every movement. Have been trained to know what every turn, slip, motion, can do. I can't pause too long, thinking I smell the lemongrass and cinnamon of her hair. How I used to wrap a ringlet around one finger as I kissed her shoulder. The scent rushed the air when she turned in her sleep, turned in my arms.

On station, the others speak around me. They want me to know they're sorry. They want me to know they would never have chosen to be told, but they don't say that part out loud. They are worried that grief will make me sloppy. They watch me like they would watch the steady beep of a monitor, waiting for the flatline.

Once while training in the NBL, submerged under tons of water, I stared up and could barely see the ceiling lights. I told her about it that night, told her about the way the weight of water never felt like anything until you tried to move after. How everything then felt heavy. She said, how strange to suddenly remember your body. What is it like to forget a body? To know the weight of someone on you, in your arms, and to lose that memory? I wondered if I could practice remembering, teach my body to hold her gone-shape like a phantom limb.

Earth comes into view as the station rotates. I wonder if I stay still too long, if I look like I'm concentrating, if they'll let me pause long enough to see where she might have been just a week before. Just a year ago. Just some time when I could go home to her. When I could wrap my arms around her, feel her heart beating, tell her I carry her when I'm an impossible distance from her. I carry. There's not enough weight out here for my arms to feel so heavy.

# Who Walks Beside You

IT BEGAN THE DAY AFTER Cameron slipped on the steps. He had had several drinks but mostly it was because of the rain. He hit his head but not hard. A single bruise shaped its way across his brow. He wasn't groggy. It didn't hurt much. He didn't think to call anyone.

At home, he took a shower, and the hot water tingled against his skin; the bruise felt like it was shimmering. He had never thought that shimmering could be a feeling, but there it was—a tingle, a shiver, a rush of warmth, a dizzying bit of light growing brighter for a second. Then he was fine. He went to bed. He slept it off.

He had a dream. It was about a woman. It was about a hallway and a woman. She was walking in front of him. Slowly in front of him. It was as if she was walking through deep water. Or maybe the dream reminded him of something somewhere in the back of his memory, left there like a single sock at the back of a closet, of the town that had been drowned in molasses, the idea of which had terrified him as a child because he couldn't stop thinking *How do you run if you can't move?* It had been the thought that ran through his head as a child when he only wanted to run and couldn't. She moved so slowly. He wanted to touch her. He reached out and touched her. She turned. Her face looked like it was the face of an angel in one of those Renaissance paintings, all light and soft angles. Her face was beautiful, except she had no eyes. In the gouged-out spaces with ragged red skin around the edges, where the eyes should have been were round white stones that had black-dot pupils painted in their centers. He stared at her, his hand still touching her skin, as she reached up and plucked the stones out. He woke up.

The morning was spent forgetting the dream. It wasn't on purpose. He just never remembered things that he dreamed. They slipped away and only sometimes would come back when he would remember things with such ferocity that he was sure that they had really happened. That afternoon he walked to work from his apartment. He always took the exact same way. It was never overly crowded and, if he had to stay late at work, it was always well lit. He had a friend who had been attacked one night while walking home from a bar. He was beaten, and three guys had kicked him over and over. The friend lost his ability to speak. Cameron didn't know if it was psychological or physical, or some twisted amalgamation of both. Cameron didn't hang out with this friend anymore. It felt strange to have a voice still, and so he felt ashamed.

Cameron knew, only a block after leaving his apartment, that there was someone following him. Maybe ten paces behind. Cameron slowed a little. He had never liked people walking behind him. It felt the same to him as when he saw a silverfish slither-crawling its way across his bathroom floor. It was a natural response. He couldn't do anything about it, but it sent jolts of anxiety up his spine. The person's pace slowed to match his. He could hear the person's footsteps; they must have been wearing flip-flops because each step seemed to be slapping exaggeratedly against the ground. Cameron wasn't exactly nervous, the day was bright outside, and cars passed by on the street every few moments, but the sensation of being followed annoyed him in a way that he couldn't quite pin down. He bent down to tie his shoes, forgetting how ridiculous the act would look since he was wearing sandals, and looked backwards. There was no one and nothing there.

At work, the day was fairly typical. He worked in a small office that did advertising for regional businesses. There were essentially two types of jobs there: the creative ones that involved designing ads and the tedious ones. Cameron didn't design ads. He left work at six and walked home alone.

Later, he went out for drinks with his friend Mark. They had known each other for years, since freshman year of college, but Cameron wouldn't necessarily call them good friends. It was more like they were acquaintances who just bumped into each other often enough that they eventually made a habit of bumping into each other. They never met outside of bars. Mark was a drinker but not a drunk. He always had a beer in his hand, Cameron pictured him casually gripping a bottle while in the delivery room of his first child or playing a round of squash. He thought that Mark would actually look strangely comical without a bottle clasped between his fingers.

The bar was crowded. It was new, having opened earlier in the month to a little bit of fanfare, and the music was too loud. They had to half-shout to hear each other. Cameron didn't necessarily think that this was a bad thing. They always talked about their jobs. Mark was an accountant at a law firm. He always told the same stories, and the lawyers in his stories always came off as buffoons. Cameron sometimes doubted the stories, not in the events that took place within them but in the way that Mark always seemed to figure out everything for the lawyers at the last possible second. Mark was in mid-rant about one of the female lawyers, a woman who he claimed he could probably have, in his terminology, on her back and legs spread at any given second, when he paused and stared at something over Cameron's shoulder. "Yo, do you know any redheads?"

Cameron considered this. He knew several redheads, and some of them were nice. He wasn't sure if Mark was looking for a hookup and he was pretty certain that he didn't want to give out any names. "Um—"

"Because there is this fine one staring at you. All come-hithery."

Cameron turned and there was a woman sitting at the opposite side of the bar with her eyes directed onto him. She was pretty. She was more than pretty. Pale skin and brilliant, fiery, yet somehow natural red hair. Cameron tried to place her. He couldn't. "I don't know her."

"Well, you should. Buy her a drink."

"Um—" Cameron began, but before he could finish articulating whatever he was trying to think up, Mark had already ordered a drink for the woman but pointed at Cameron when he was buying it.

"You're too much of a pussy, Cam."

Cameron shrugged. It was the best defense against accusations of being a coward. He liked to appear indifferent. This had been a strategy that had gotten him through years of living with his father, a man who felt that men were only truly men if they were wearing lettermen jackets and pushing people into walls. Men weren't allowed to scream.

The drink was brought to the woman, and she smiled at Cameron. Her smile was familiar to him, like something out of a dream that he had had once, or sort of like an illustration of the Cheshire Cat that he had seen as a kid. The smile was too white and too big and too even. Cameron didn't like the smile. It made the woman suddenly less than beautiful. "She's not my type, Mark."

"That woman is every guy's type. Or wait, are you finally coming out?" Mark's sense of humor had always been the kind that edged quickly to bullying. This had never really bothered Cameron. Mark without that edge of meanness would have hardly had enough personality to qualify as a person.

"Why don't you go talk to her?" Cameron asked. He figured Mark couldn't resist a challenge.

"I will." Mark walked over to the woman, beer bottle dangling from one hand, and began talking as soon as he reached her. Cameron ordered another beer. He stared down into the bottle and caught a glimpse of his eye reflected up at him. In the reflection his eye flooded with blackness, as if his pupil had exploded.

Cameron rushed to the bathroom to look in the mirror. His eyes both looked fine, maybe a little redder than usual, as if he had been about to cry. He peered closer at his reflection. He was thirty but looked at least ten years older all of a sudden. He examined the bruise on his forehead. It had gone the color of a too-ripe plum and made the frown lines on his brow seem deeper and more pronounced. He leaned closer to the window, and behind him something moved. It was a small click of sound, like one of the stall doors had opened just the tiniest of cracks. Cameron didn't turn around but looked in the mirror to see if there was someone there. There wasn't. Or there was no one that he could see. The sound again, this time a little louder, and with a creak to it, as if one of the doors was being slowly opened. Still he saw nothing. He turned to face the doors. They were all closed. He left the bathroom.

He went back to where they had been sitting, but Mark was nowhere around. The woman with the red, red hair was gone as well. Cameron decided to go home. He figured that Mark maybe was as good as his talk, or maybe he had wanted it to seem that way at least. Cameron didn't want to take that away from him.

He only lived about four blocks away and it wasn't too late, so he chose to walk. He was two blocks away from his apartment when he again felt that there was someone behind him. It wasn't even by sound. It was just a sense. He sped up. The follower sped up. By the time Cameron reached his apartment he was sprinting.

He, not for the first time, felt a surge of love and hatred toward the building's security door. Hatred because he had to spend a few seconds fumbling with his keys and then love when he felt the door click shut behind him. He went up to his apartment and locked himself in.

He couldn't understand why the moment had gotten to him. Cameron generally considered himself a calm person. There had been the day years before when he had come home to find his father lying on the living room floor and Cameron hadn't panicked. His mother had been there too, staring at Cameron as if willing him to be the one to act. Cameron remembered that he had nodded. Even in that situation he had nodded, that single nod of his to show his mother that he was all right. Then he had simply walked to the phone and dialed an ambulance. If there had been anything uncalm in him, it had been in the way that he walked a good ten feet around the body, afraid to go too close in case his father might suddenly sit straight up, laughing because he was only playing a little joke on Cameron. A little joke. That's what his father always called them.

Cameron took a shower and let the water get too hot. It tattooed his skin with red, vaguely unformed blotches across his entire body. He fell asleep with his skin still giving off waves of warmth.

He had a dream that he was falling. He was at the top of a flight of stairs and someone pushed him from behind. The funny thing was that as he fell, he wasn't falling backwards. He fell upwards toward the ceiling and then through it. The ceiling wasn't hard, it was like whipped cream and he kept sinking upwards until he was free of the ceiling and the house and everything. He fell through the sky. It was night. The stars were waves of color, and they blinked around him. In and out. In and out like Christmas lights set on a cycle of flashing. Like fireflies sending Morse code out to their lovers. Like a cardiogram sending up shivering signs of life. Then the stars solidified and opened up around him, the stars became mouths. They became filled with teeth. And then they devoured him. Cameron woke up.

His phone buzzed to wake him. Cameron reached out and grabbed it. A text from Mark. *That chick was wild.* It took Cameron a full five minutes before he realized what Mark could have been talking about. He texted back: *The redhead?* Mark responded within a second: *Ya. U missed out.* Cameron tried to come up with a response that would fully satisfy Mark, the best he could come up with was: *Aw damn.* He got out of bed.

As he brushed his teeth, he noticed how the bruise had become tinged with green. It looked like a ripe eggplant slowly reverting back to its unripe stage. He spat out his toothpaste, and only noticed that it was tinged red with blood as he rinsed it down the sink. He spat again. Blood filled his saliva. He looked into the mirror, opening his mouth as widely as he could, and noticed that he must have bitten the inside of his cheek in his sleep. The normally pink flesh was ragged and red. He wondered how he hadn't woken up from the pain.

He was running a few minutes late, so he speed-walked to work. Again, he was sure that there was someone walking behind him, but a little closer than before. He took out his cell phone and looked into it, hoping to use the screen as a mirror. He had seen *Clash of the Titans* as a child and had been overly impressed with Perseus's cunning use of the shield to facedown Medusa. He saw a person reflected in his phone. He couldn't tell if it was a man or a woman. There was something about the body that suggested a man, but something about the walk that suggested a woman. He thought of that Kinks song but in reverse: *She drank champagne but it tasted like cherry cola.* His phone was too dark and too smudged to make out the person's face. He thought about turning but then thought against it. He thought that seeing his stalker would be somehow worse than just knowing that he or she were there. He remembered once hiding under his bed. He knew his father was in his room, could hear his footsteps punching against the ground, but Cameron just kept his eyes closed until the sound went away. Until everything went away.

His phone rang as he was looking into it and he nearly dropped it. "Hello?"

"Hi, sweetie." It was his mother. He almost sighed with relief. His mother had a way of taking away his fear. Her voice was like clean beds and hot cocoa and safety.

"Hey, Mom."

"I know you're probably on your way to work, but I just wanted to hear your voice. I had the strangest dream about you."

"A dream?" Cameron slowed his steps.

"You were you but younger and not how you were when you actually were younger."

"Yeah, that's not confusing, Mom." He tried to smile, hoping that she could hear his smile across phone signals.

"It was like how you would have been as a child if you had been happier." She sounded sad. She sounded as if she were standing on a mountain looking out across a city set to flame and there was no way to ever find enough water to save it all.

"Mom, I was happy. You always made sure of that." He felt like crying. He felt like running. He remembered the way his father's body looked in a casket, so emptied out of cruelty. Maybe, he had thought, the dead look kinder in death.

"I just wish you had always been happy." They spent a few moments in silence. Then he told her that he loved her and they said their goodbyes. Cameron put his phone away. He couldn't hear anyone walking behind him anymore. The person must have turned off or gone into a shop.

At work, he stayed late without thinking about it. He left when one of his coworkers was also leaving late, a woman who had never really talked to him but always seemed friendly. She had a scar that ran down her cheek, which Cameron had been told by another coworker was the result of an assault. Cameron had been unable to look at the woman properly since hearing this. His eyes always wanted to shift toward the scar and find some reason that someone could be so hurt nestled into the patterns of ruined skin.

"Hey, Cameron. How are you?" she asked, smiling.

"Okay, what about you?"

"Good, good. I noticed that someone's been walking to work with you, the past couple of days." She didn't mean anything by it. She was making conversation.

Cameron didn't know what to say. "Walking with me?"

"Yeah, the past few days, the person who walks beside you?"

"I, um, it must be a coincidence." Cameron could feel a shake starting in his body. A tremor running up his spine.

"Oh, okay. I thought . . ." She shook her head, smiled again. "Never mind. Have a nice night, Cameron."

"You too." His voice wasn't shaking, but he knew that the shaking would start soon. His voice hadn't done this in years. He had once been unable to speak for hours at a time, the shaking consuming his throat as if it were swelling up inside of him. This hadn't happened in years.

He walked home as quickly as he could. His phone buzzed. Mark wanted to get drinks. Cameron thought that maybe drinks would be good. A little calm for his body. A little bit of warmth to shake the chill that had been creeping up on him. He changed direction and walked to the bar instead.

He ordered a drink and was halfway through it by the time that Mark got there. "So that girl was crazy. She was into stuff that even I didn't know."

"Redheads, huh?" Cameron offered.

"Like wildfire." Mark raised his eyebrows, smiled.

"So I guess she just wanted anyone last night. Wasn't staring at me at all."

"Just wanted to get fucked. Too bad you didn't offer." Mark had a beer already in hand. Cameron wondered if Mark had brought it in with him because he hadn't even seen him order one.

"Have you ever thought that you might be losing your mind?" Cameron asked. He hadn't meant to ask.

"Never, bud, never." Mark said and then he looked more carefully at Cameron and for the first time ever his face turned serious. "Cameron, are you okay, man?"

"Yeah. It's just that I keep thinking there's someone following me."

"Really? That's weird, actually. Because when I arrived here, I could have sworn someone was standing right behind you. I was gonna ask who it was . . ."

"What did they look like?"

"It's funny, but I can't remember." Mark looked around as if he might spot the person in the crowd and be able to point them out. "So, maybe you're not going crazy . . ."

"That's somehow not reassuring," Cameron said.

"Sorry, man." Mark shrugged as if this were something that could be shrugged away.

Cameron suddenly wondered about something he had never wondered about before: Mark's childhood. Had it been a good one?

Had he had a life that was unremarkable and so was peaceful? "Hey, man, do you get along with your parents?"

Mark paused for a second before answering. "Weird leap, but yeah, I do. Why?"

"I was just thinking that I don't really know anything about your life before we met in college. Isn't that weird? I've known you for over a decade and I know nothing about your family."

"We're just not the type that talk about that shit." Another shrug. Childhoods, families, lives, shrugged away. Mark didn't ask about Cameron's family. Cameron was glad. They stared into their drinks. "So, like, that lawyer chick I was talking about. She told me that if I keep talking to her, she's going to get me fired for harassment. Can you believe that?"

They talked for a while longer. Drank a few more rounds. Cameron walked home, though Mark offered to drive him. The evenings were starting to get chilly. It was in the beginning of fall, and leaves rustled on the trees around him. He thought the rustling would be easy to confuse for shuffling footsteps. He thought that the footsteps behind him would be easy to confuse for his heartbeat. It pounded in his chest. They pounded on the ground. If hearts that could pound so heavily with life could stop, then surely a single set of footsteps pounding behind him could stop as well. Later, he watched the TV and finally fell asleep on the couch. He dreamed of his father sitting at the dinner table eating a bowl of something. Cameron felt small as he walked to his father and tapped him on the shoulder. His father turned slowly and his mouth was black. He was eating a bowl of dirt, worms writhing in it, and bits of twigs and dead leaves stuck in as well. Cameron backed away. He felt a pain overcome his head. Something like a migraine but worse. It felt like everything was being pulled apart and pushed together at the same time. In the pain came the memory of the first time his father hit him. It was with the full force of the back of his hand and across the front of Cameron's face. The bruise had stayed for weeks across his forehead, a stain, and he had had to come up with excuse after excuse. He had fallen, he said. He had just fallen in his yard and hit the edge of the porch. Each time the lie got more elaborate. It was a beginner's mistake. He learned quickly to make the lies simple. People liked the ability to hear the lie and be able to believe it. To not have to ask questions. Cameron remembered the bruise that first time, his father saying it was as ugly as Cameron.

He woke up to silence. He woke up to dark. He woke up to the way the apartment crowded around him even though he was the only one there. Cameron got up off of the couch. He left his apartment. It was the middle of the night, and the street was empty and silent. He began to walk. The footsteps started behind him. Closer than ever. The person was right behind his shoulder. Cameron turned around and faced the nothing.

# Out in the Dark

THERE WAS NOTHING. ONLY SILENCE and sterility. Everything so clean. Sleek. Emptied. Sometimes Olivia counted the buttons on the control panel. She counted them all or sometimes she counted them by color or by function and sub-function. On some days, she looked out the window, remembering back to when she first saw the view and thought that there was no way anyone would ever get used to it. Sometimes she would practice holding her breath, seeing how long she could go. It was one way to fill the empty time.

She'd gotten used to the view. If there was a flame going past, or an explosion of distant objects, she knew that she'd be terrified but also secretly thrilled. The thrill would race up her spine and play at the base of her skull. It'd feel like rollercoasters or driving too fast around sharp curves in the road. For a second, she'd be happy, joyful, truly ecstatic with the destruction.

It had been seven months. Only hours left and then she'd dock. It was a routine circumnavigation. Olivia wasn't even sure exactly why she'd been sent. The mission could have been done by anyone, it could have been done by *anything*, if she really had to say. Her function there was as uselessly outdated as an appendix. The pod was the one taking the photos, recording whatever it was that needed to be preserved. For posterity? Was that a saying? Preserved for posterity? And if it was, what did it mean? Olivia had thought every thought possible, she was fairly certain, over the course of the past seven months. She might never have an original thought again, having already pondered it at some point during the voyage. *Voyage* seemed too grand a word. She circled. She flew through the darkness, through the stars, and all she was doing was rotating. Round and round. It was enough to make her occasionally burst into laughter. Laughter had a frightening edge to it when everything else was silence, when there were no witnesses to hear it.

The darkness was something she hadn't expected. She was used to night skies. They too were dark, but their darkness was filled with sound and motion—the chorus of spring peepers, the soft vibrating buzz of bat wings swooping overhead, the rustle of wind through trees. Somehow, they made the dark less dark.

The darkness out there, out all around her, was punctuated by

distant stars and planets—lights were turning on and off somewhere out there—but it seemed an immoveable and impenetrable
darkness. Olivia couldn't imagine the light ever coming. In space,
the darkness was forever.

Olivia hummed songs under her breath at first. There were ones
she remembered the tunes to, ones she remembered the words
to, and ones she wondered if she had simply made up. Eventually,
they sounded too harsh amid the silence, amid the enclosing black
around her.

She dreamed in heavy slumbers, the dreams often only blurs
of colors and lights. She woke and lost the dream worlds quickly.
They slipped away from her, no matter how she tried to grasp
onto them—like when she had tried to carry the ocean back in her
hands to show her mother, the water slipping between her fingers
no matter how tightly she thought she had them pressed together.
*Mom, I*—but in her hands there was nothing, just the feeling of
having once held something vast. The dreams began to fall away.
She dreamed of the darkness outside the windows. It was her most
recent memory. Sometimes her only memory, the darkness tapping
against the window, slipping in. All around her, all of the time.

Olivia blinked, hearing her breaths going in and out, in and
out, in and out. She opened her eyes and saw it. The station was in
front of her. She was so close. She breathed in and out.

The station seemed to shine and glisten, so bright amid the
darkness, almost hurting her eyes. The pod slipped into docking
and, though the motion was barely a motion, she fell over. Her
stomach jumped like she was on an elevator, plunging so fast as to
only mean death.

The view screen came to life. It had been so long since it had
buzzed with an image that she stared at it for a moment in open-
mouthed awe. She had forgotten that there was a way for them to
contact her. There had been a way for them to contact her. When
had it last been? Around month three? Could it have been that
long? Did they forget she was out there?

"Please identify yourself." The voice crisp, cool. The face was a
man, stern.

"Olivia Ross. I'm back from the recording navigation. I'm back."
Her voice sounded strained to her, scratchy and underused. She
wanted some water, so parched.

The man on the screen looked down at something, probably information on another screen, so many screens, before looking up again. "Welcome back. Someone will meet you at the bay doors."

"Thank you. Thank you." Olivia couldn't hide the desperate glee in her voice.

The screen went black. Something shifted outside. The docking bay doors. Olivia felt movement. Then words flashed on the screen. She was cleared to open the pod. The doors took only seconds to slide open, but Olivia would've sworn on her life that they creaked and shuddered and stalled. The docking bay was barely lit, only one row of track lighting, and it was devoid of movement. Olivia remembered her first time seeing it—everyone scurried about and she had thought of those things that parents were always buying for science-minded children, the ant environments or whatever they were called. Olivia had had one as a little girl, and she had been entranced by the ants shuffling along between the two sheets of plastic. She'd recorded their daily routines in a notebook. At night, she read them stories and hoped that her parents didn't over-hear. The stories were often about brave knights. She wondered which heroes ants told stories about.

One morning, she woke up and discovered the ants moving more slowly. She put them in the sunlight hoping to warm them back into bustling. Within hours the ants began to die. She used her microscope to study one of the dead, zooming in closer and closer, there appeared to be tiny threads woven in and out of the body. A fungus of some sort, her father told her, and then thrown the case out with the trash. Later, Olivia dug the plastic case from the garbage and gave the ants a burial. They deserved that much at least. Knights were always laid to rest properly. The docking bay now reminded her of nothing so much as that emptied-out plastic case. Once it had been so full of movement that it made the wrong-ness of its stillness seem even more sinister.

Olivia took a step out. It felt odd to be free of the pod, like floating, and she didn't know if she liked the feeling or not. Her legs wobbled beneath her. The doors on the far end of the bay slid open. There was someone there.

"Olivia?" The voice was one she knew. Chris. Someone she'd call a friend. Someone who left her out alone and spinning in silence for however long it had been since they last contacted her.

"Yeah. Chris?"

He walked toward her. His pace fast, one speed below running. "Olivia. Jesus, you were out there all this time."

She stopped moving toward him. "Of course I was. Where else would I have been?"

He was near to her now and she could see how drawn his face looked, how worn down. "You could have been dead. We thought you were dead."

"What? Why?"

"We lost your feed. You were there one moment and then it went out. Months ago. We thought there had been a malfunction. We thought . . . and then when everyone started getting sick, we thought maybe you had gotten sick as well." Chris studied her. His gaze moving over her inch-by-inch, as if double-checking that she was real.

"What sickness?" Olivia wanted to lie down, to stare at walls around her that were not the walls of the pod.

"We don't know. Two-thirds of the station came down with it." Chris stopped speaking for a moment. "Maybe we should fill you in on it tomorrow. Let you get your bearings back."

There was something in his voice, a tightness, like he was trying to hold some words down, deep in his throat. Olivia needed to hear whatever it was. There was something, and it needed to be let out. "What is it? Is it bad?"

"About half the crew is dead. The other portion that got sick are in some kind of coma."

"A coma?"

He nodded, swallowing hard. Olivia realized what it was—Chris was fighting back tears. Maybe of sadness or worry or fear, but tears all the same. "Jesus, what's causing it? Where did it come from?"

He shook his head. Olivia wanted to ask a thousand questions but couldn't bring herself to speak. It had been months since she had spoken to anyone, months since she had seen someone cry. She didn't want to see someone cry. "Can we get out of the dock?"

He nodded and almost took her arm as if to lead her. His hand reached for her elbow before dropping back down to his side. They walked out of the docking bay. The doors whooshed open and they stepped into a hallway. Again, it was eerily emptied of life. Knowing the reason behind the emptiness didn't make it better.

Chris led her to the room she had once bunked in. She had shared it with three others. There had been Rachel and Naya and Sofia. How many were dead? The words would not form on her tongue to ask. The door slid open, and Olivia looked in before stepping inside. The beds were all neatly made up, the blankets tucked in, hospital corners tight. Olivia stepped inside the room. Her bed had been the top bunk on the left side. She walked to it. There were still her things put up on the wall next to the bed. The pictures she had always looked at before falling asleep.

"Are . . ." She couldn't finish the question.

"Yes," Chris answered. The question hadn't been needed. It was the only thing she could have possibly asked.

Olivia walked to the bunk. Was she going to be allowed to sleep right away? Weren't there procedures? Weren't there reports she had to file? Supervisors she would have to talk to? She turned to Chris. "Am I supposed to report in?"

He shook his head. "We'll brief you after you get some rest."

It felt odd. Wrong. She reached out a hand toward him, unsure of why she was doing it. "Chris?"

Chris looked away from her and closed the door. It whooshed closed. She went up to it and pressed all of the buttons. The door was locked. It was a mistake. Olivia banged a fist against the door. Once. "Chris!"

There was nothing. Silence. The door stayed closed, locked, impenetrable. She shouted, though she knew that no one could hear her through the door. "What's going on?"

She moved back to the bunk. She climbed up and lay down on her old bed. She might as well rest. Everything would be explained. Some new protocol. Or Chris didn't know the doors would lock behind him. There was an explanation. The pictures on her wall caught the light and shimmered for a moment.

There was a picture of the lake near her house. A picture of her sister. Of her dog. Of her best friend. Their names. They had names. The lake was Lake Scàil. Pronounced like *squirrel* but not quite, her mother used to tell people. Skaw-il. Skaw-il. Her sister was Ophelia. Her dog was Ovid. It was a joke. She couldn't remember the joke. Best friend. Best friend. Best friend.

Olivia woke up to darkness. For a second, she thought she was back in the pod. Her heart thudding against her ribcage, she silently begged her lungs to take air in. It had been a dream, and the darkness was back, around her, embracing her, prepared to hold her again forever. Then her eyes adjusted to the darkness. She was on her bunk, alone in the room. She climbed down. She tried to feel for the light controls. A single light flickered on, tinged with green. Had the lights always been this bad? This buzzy and flickering and green? It made her feel like she was in some underwater cave, just a little light filtering down through algae-infested water. The other bunks were empty. Rachel's had a picture of her husband pinned by it. What had they told him? What message had been relayed to him? What do people back on earth do when there isn't just no body but no chance of a body? Olivia thought of men buried at sea and of the widows who would have just learned that their husbands were gone. Did they spend years nightmaring about bodies slipping into the sea, slipping beneath the waves, disappearing?

A knocking. A knocking on the door, and Olivia jumped. The door began to open. There was someone standing in the doorway wearing a full suit of protective gear. Olivia calculated escape—her chances of knocking the person down, of sprinting to the docking bay, of reaching her pod without anyone catching her. She caught herself calculating and let the shock sink in. Why did she need to escape? Why did her body scream out for escape?

"Olivia. It's Doctor Transom. I'm wearing this suit as a protective measure." Doctor Transom. Smooth, deep voice. It registered somewhere in Olivia's mind.

"Why? Protect against what?"

"Olivia. We don't know why the epidemic started. We don't know if you've been infected. Some people on the station, like Chris, seem to have immunity. I don't, as far as I know, and I'd rather not be infected if you're a carrier."

"How could I be a carrier? I wasn't even here when it started." Olivia felt her body trembling.

"We don't know the cycle of this disease. You could have been exposed as soon as you came back on the ship. We have to take every precautionary measure." Doctor Transom took a step toward Olivia, and she took a step backward.

"Olivia, I'm not going to hurt you. I'm going to escort you to the lab. I just want to run some blood tests." Smooth, deep, calming voice.

Olivia walked toward the doctor. Transom took her arm gently, but there was a firmness, a tightness to the grip of his hand around her wrist, as if he was preparing to lead an unruly child. Olivia followed him toward the lab. The halls were still empty. There was such silence. It was the silence of the darkness.

The lab doors opened. Whoosh. Transom led her to a chair and Olivia sat down in it. "How many died?"

Transom was preparing a needle. "It was about half. More, I think, if we're going to be precise. Then there is another, a quarter, almost a third, in coma."

"How many got sick and recovered?"

She laid her arm out flat. Transom snapped a band around her upper arm, feeling for a vein with two gloved fingertips. "Nobody recovered, Olivia. Anyone who got it is either in a coma or dead."

The needle went in. It hurt with an intensity that Olivia could barely remember. How long had it been since she felt pain? There'd been no pain in the pod. Her toes curled with the stabbing ache and she tried not to make a sound.

"How did everyone else not get it?"

Transom did not speak. They both watched the blood filling the vial. Dark red and thick. Was blood always so thick? Thicker than water. Was that a saying? Were all sayings so obvious? Olivia felt laughter curling up her throat.

"We don't know. Some like Chris were exposed but didn't get any symptoms. Some of us avoided exposure. We don't know how it works."

"Have you done autopsies? What—"

Transom cut off Olivia's words. "Chris didn't tell you?"

Transom unsnapped the band. Olivia stared at the tiny mark on her arm. "Tell me what?"

"The bodies. As soon as people died, they disintegrated as soon as they were touched. That's when they are most contagious as well. The bodies turn to dust, and the dust seems to be what spreads the sickness."

Transom turned, holding the vial. Olivia felt nauseous; she wanted to vomit out the images that began to appear in her mind. "Jesus, Jesus. What about the ones in the coma?"

"They seem fine. Their vitals are stable. They just won't wake up."

Transom was running her blood through an analysis. Olivia watched the numbers and symbols popping up on the screen. They seemed to glow. "It looks like you're clean."

"There's a way to test for it?"

"Yes and no. Some anomalies popped up in the blood work of people when they were first exposed." Transom turned back to Olivia.

She thought she should feel relief. She thought she should have felt something. She felt nothing. "What's going to happen?"

Transom didn't say anything. He walked over to a panel on the far wall. He pressed a button and spoke into the panel. "She's clear."

"Transom, what's going to happen?"

"What was it like out there for so long without anyone?" he asked.

Olivia remembered the darkness and the silence all around her, squirming between her ears and nestling into her eyes. The darkness had swallowed her up, and she had rested in the mouth of nothing. "What's going to happen?"

"I imagine it was peaceful. Was it? No one else around that you had to take care of, no voices you had to answer to. There was just you, and you were all."

Olivia looked at the door. It was five feet away. She could make it to the door. She could make it through the door. Something was wrong. She stood up. The door opened. Whoosh. There were two people there. They wore the protective suits. They came to her and each took one of her arms. "Transom. You said I was clear."

Transom turned to her. He nodded. "You're clear."

"What's happening?"

The two around her began to move. She was being taken away. "Doctor! Doctor!"

Transom looked away from her. She thought to struggle, but what was the point? She walked along. "Where are you taking me?"

They didn't speak, and without voices they were just bodies moving. The protective masks concealed their faces. She probably knew them. They had probably had conversations, told jokes, swapped family names. They led her to a room and pushed her inside. It was dark. It was dark. She knew the dark. The doors closed.

She stepped back, bumping into something. It was a shape she knew. There was a body in the room with her. She stepped away from it. A light flickered on. A woman's body on the floor. She looked perfect. Asleep. Except there was a certain golden quality to her skin, a goldenness that didn't look quite living.

"Olivia, we're sorry." Transom's voice came through the audio panel. Smooth and deep. "We need to solve this crisis. The next supply ship is on its way. We need to solve this so we can go home."

"What does it have to do with me?"

"We need to study it from its inception. We haven't studied the disease from its beginning. We were trying to draw straws, you know?" He laughed. He actually laughed, relieved. "We were trying to decide who would volunteer to be tested on. It was so hard, there were so many arguments. And then you came back, miraculously alive and back to dock. You must see how divine that is? You returned to save us."

Olivia stared at the body on the floor. She thought of the darkness and how it had drained through the pod windows every time she closed her eyes. It had swept over and around her. The first day without voices, and she had tried so hard to call them up. The control buttons. She had pressed them. She had pressed them, jabbing with her fingers until her fingertips were bruised. She had sobbed and pleaded. They had forgotten her, she had thought. She had tried to think of the lake and the shadows and her sister and her dog and her parents and the lake and the lake.

"Maybe we can cure you too, Olivia. Maybe we can cure you too."

She looked at where she had bumped into the body. The woman's leg. There was something moving inside the body. Olivia stared and tried not to stare. No, it wasn't something moving. It was the body collapsing in on itself. She had bumped the body.

The darkness had embraced her. It had held her for months. Olivia had dreamed at first of home. She had dreamed of swimming. Of water and light. Eventually though, even her dreams had been of the darkness.

The body was sinking into itself. The features of the woman's face fell inward, erasing her beauty. Olivia had once been walking in the woods and had stepped onto a puffball mushroom past its prime.

The mushroom had deflated, like a beach ball punctured. This is what she thought of as she watched the woman's face. Through the thin lines of light, Olivia saw it, tiny dust particles floating up off of the body, into the air. Idiots, she thought, it wasn't dust. It was spores. She held her breath. She held her breath. The darkness had taught her how to wait in stillness, how to hold her breath and let the night fill her.

"Olivia, you have now been exposed for a sufficient amount of time. This isn't about hurting you. You don't need to be terrorized. You must understand this. We are going to open the doors. Please make your way out. You are doing this for all of us."

The doors opened and Olivia raced out into the hallway. The two stood sentinel. They watched her, faces still hidden by the masks. She wondered if Chris was one of them. They each took one of her arms. They led her first to the shower room, let her stand under the hot water and rinse off her skin. She watched the water go down her body in rivulets. She allowed herself to finally take a breath. She could feel her blood moving just below her skin. For a moment, she thought she could see the darkness crawling through her veins beneath the flesh. She stepped out from beneath the water.

They led her to the sick bay. The doors opened. Whoosh.

There were so many beds, and upon each lay a person. They could have been sleeping. Olivia stared at them. There were so many. They led her to an empty bed. She laid down upon it without fuss.

"The doctor will be here soon. The doors will lock behind us. Wait here." One of the suits said. It had a voice. Olivia tried to remember the voice. A man, she could tell, but soft-voiced.

They walked away. She watched them. The doors opened. Whoosh. They stepped outside. The doors closed. Whoosh. Olivia sat up on the bed. She stepped onto the floor and walked over to the closest sleeping body. It was Sofia, her bunkmate. Or it had been Sofia.

"What are you now? What's growing up inside you?" Olivia asked in a whisper. After the ants died, she had studied different sorts of fungi. There were so many. The parasitic ones were the ones that terrified her. She had imagined them, sometimes, as she slept. The threads spooling into her lungs. "Wake up. Wake up. I want to see you."

The body did not stir. Olivia walked back to her cot. She laid down. She closed her eyes. The darkness spooled out, its fingers playing in her hair. The darkness was all around. She opened her eyes to pitch blackness. She stayed lying down. There were others moving around her though. Sounds of feet stepping down from beds, of soft shuffling steps. They moved as one to the door. She wondered if they'd notice her, but they walked past her. The darkness lay on her like a blanket. She was a child hiding in her bed, and the monsters couldn't see her.

A knocking on the door. It opened. Whoosh. One of the suits, holding a flashlight. The beam splayed across the standing bodies. They flinched from the light. The suit said one word, or almost-word, a sound, before they swarmed around him or her.

Olivia listened. The noises were so loud they scraped inside her head, aching in her eardrums. There had been silence before. She had known silence.

The bodies swarmed into the hallway. It was pitch dark. The flashlight beam was cast along the floor from where the flashlight had rolled into a corner. Olivia stepped out of the bed and walked toward the door. She didn't need the light. She knew the darkness. She walked into the hallway, making her way toward the docking bay. There were screams and shouts from elsewhere. Such noise.

Olivia came to the docking-bay doors. She pressed the button and the doors opened. Whoosh. That horrible aching sound. She walked to the pods. Each would be filled with supplies. They were for safety. They were for exploration. They were ready.

She stepped into one. She knew the controls well. Her hands still held their memory like a violinist who has given up music for years but can still play a song if asked. Finger memory. Touch.

The pod felt so close around her. There had been things in another life. How far away was her home? How many months? She had done it before. She could do it again. Skaw-il. Water. Was it dark at the bottom of a lake? Could the light get down there? Was it possible to stare up through all that water and see the sun still?

It would be months, but she was fine. The darkness would keep her safe. The darkness would keep her warm. It crept through the windows and rested itself around her. She wore the darkness, and it wore her.

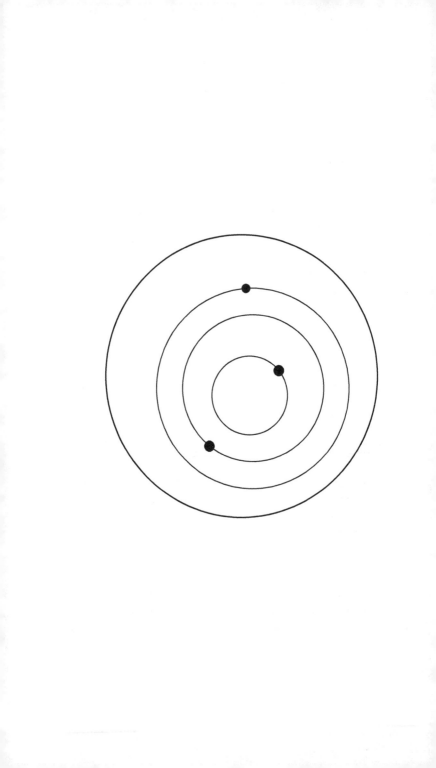

# Simultaneity

SHE THINKS OFTEN OF HER father. He goes to space and comes back and does not go again. Her mother, while washing dishes and talking to a friend on the phone, says something about her father's time in space. *He'll never tell me. Something happened though. The way he looks at the sky, when he thinks no one's watching. It's like he longs for it and he's terrified of it.* Angeline asks her father if he misses space. He shakes his head and says that space is too far from her. She likes that answer. When talking at her father's funeral, she thinks of it and starts crying. Not only because she misses him, but because she finally realizes that it may not be the complete truth.

When Angeline is young, she thinks she wants to follow in the footsteps of her grandfather, to go into the sea, to study the depths of water. At age fifteen though, she nearly drowns after a misjudged dive into a pool. Spitting water onto concrete, gasping for breath, she feels a different sort of fear than she's ever felt before. It's a fear not of monsters or teenage embarrassment, but rather a fear that her body can be broken. That all bodies can be broken.

When Angeline first goes into space, she thinks of her mother's paintings. Her mother's art is often of gardens. Not pretty ones, but rather ones left desolate, barren, fountains cracked, birds pecking among rotting fruit. But when her mother paints, she smiles, laughs, looks happier than at any other moment. It is like she is letting the darkness seep from inside her onto the canvas. Angeline makes the connection only years later, how space can also be a collection of darkness and shadows.

When Angeline sees the world flying up at her, she tries not to blink. There is something beautiful there, though she tries and fails to put her finger on it. She wonders if her life will flash before her eyes. She wonders if she would have changed anything. She remembers her mother painting, her father speaking, the sea, the sea. She remembers the way water looks when the sun is almost down and the light hits waves and everything shimmers and shines.

Angeline, go to sleep, her father says from the doorway. Tomorrow he leaves, goes into a spaceship and up into the sky. He comes back. He is different. Space changes everyone. Angeline says, tell me a story. Once upon a time.

Her mother cries at her father's funeral. She doesn't speak, and so Angeline speaks and her voice shakes and she thinks, how did I get so old? Where is my father? He was just right here.

# Wearing the Body

"WHAT'S THE TRICK?" SHE asked as she leaned forward in her chair. Her blouse dipped as she did so, revealing the slopes of her breasts and the necklace that hung between them. It was a pendant, shaped like a half-lidded eye. The pupil was a tiny black pearl.

Conor shifted back in his own seat, away from her closeness, from her need. "It's a card trick. It tells a story if you lay it down right."

"What story does it tell?" She reached out, as if to touch his knee, as she asked. Conor tried not to flinch.

"Whatever story you need it to," he said.

"Will you show it to me? Will you show me the trick?" Her voice was a plea. Her voice was a beggar asking for a single coin to save her life.

He nodded. He had never been able not to when faced with such need. And they always had such need.

He gathered up his card deck, riffle-shuffled it, nothing flashy. He handed it to her and told her to cut the deck as many times as she liked. She cut it once, carefully. She seemed to be trying to measure the deck exactly into two halves. She handed the deck back to him, hands trembling, tiny earthquakes of loss.

He began to tell the story. It was always the same story, really, though he changed the names and the circumstances. It was always the same story.

CONOR WAS BORN ON A Sunday. His parents were religious in a way that leaned more toward superstition than grace. They thought he'd be the blessed child. They thought he'd make everything better. He did, at first. He was a smiling baby, an early laugher. His first full sentence was *I want a joke*. He liked to dance as a toddler, wobbling on chubby legs to whatever music came on the radio. He was happy. His parents were happy.

When he was seven, he met his first dead person, and then everything changed. Though it wasn't all at once; it wasn't as dramatic as everyone would make believe in the stories normally told about these sorts of things.

She sat in the branches of a tree, swinging her legs and humming to herself. He was walking past, saw her and waved. She waved back, and he saw how her hand was made of leaves. Dead leaves formed together to make a palm and five fingers. He stared, though he knew it wasn't polite to do so.

"Whatcha looking at?" she asked.

"Your hand, how did it get that way? Did you have an accident?" At that age he always pronounced it *ax-ee-dent*.

The girl smiled. "You could say that, kiddo."

"Why did the doctors fix it like that?" he asked. He knew his mother would have scolded him for his questions. But his mother wasn't there.

The girl took a few moments before answering. "The Doctor fixes things with what she can."

He nodded as if this made perfect sense. Conor had never liked to seem that he didn't know what was going on. "Oh."

"It's not so bad, kiddo. I can climb trees much better now than I ever could before," the girl said. She climbed higher up into the tree as if to prove this to him. It was true. She barely seemed to be climbing at all, as if the tree bent its branches closer to her and she simply stepped upward. Conor gaped. He wished he were that good at climbing trees.

The girl laughed down at him. "See, the Doctor tries to make things better. She really does."

"Which doctor is she?" he asked. He wondered if this doctor worked with his family doctor, the stern Dr. Griss who always said that Conor shouldn't squirm so much when he was getting his shots.

"You'll know her when you meet her," the girl replied. She disappeared higher into the tree and Conor could no longer see her through all of the leaves. He waited a few minutes, but when the girl didn't reappear, he decided he had better get home before his mother worried.

He told his mother about the girl. "She had hands made of leaves, Mama!"

His mother smiled, a mother-smile. "Of course she did, Conor. And was she a fairy?"

He thought about this for a moment. "No, I don't think so. She was wearing a yellow jumper and blue tennis shoes."

His mother paused in what she was doing, cutting carrots, the sharp click of the knife stopped and the room was quiet. "A yellow jumper and blue tennis shoes?"

He nodded. He was finishing a snack at the table, peanut butter and raspberry jam on bread. He took a bite of the sandwich and a little jam squirted out onto the table. His mother stared at the blob of jam as if it was an inkblot test and she needed to see the right thing in order to be found sane.

"That's . . ." She didn't finish what she was going to say. She walked out of the room and then returned with the newspaper. She laid it down on the table next to Conor. "Conor, did you see this paper this morning before school?"

He shook his head. He wondered why his mother could possibly have thought that he might look at the newspaper. Even the cartoons in the newspaper were boring.

She pointed at the front page. There was a picture of a girl, she was wearing a yellow jumper and blue tennis shoes. "Is that the girl you saw?"

He looked at the picture. It was the girl, except in the photo she had both hands. "Yes, but she doesn't have the funny hand there."

His mother stared at him. He looked up at his mother, and for the first time he saw something in her eyes that could only be called fear.

THEY WENT TO SEE HIS grandmother. They almost never did. There was the perfunctory visit at holidays, but his mother always bustled them back out practically the moment they arrived. His grandmother's house was always kept dark and cool, like the snake area of the pet stores. His grandmother, herself reminded him not of a snake but of a lizard. She curled in things, usually her sitting chair, and her gaze darted around the room every few moments. She always held her hands in fists, fingers curling and uncurling as if she were working an invisible stress ball.

"Mother, he saw one, I think he saw one," were his mother's first words to her mother as they stepped inside the house.

His grandmother looked at him closely and motioned for them to sit. His mother went to the couch and he followed her, though he had never liked sitting on that couch. It gave away too easily and he always sunk into it; he sometimes had nightmares of it swallowing him whole.

"So, Conor, you saw a Dead One?" his grandmother asked.

"A what?" he asked.

"A Dead One. A spirit," she replied.

"No, I saw a girl. She had a hand made of leaves. She was in a tree." He was matter-of-fact. He knew what he'd seen. She had been a most thoroughly alive girl. He had seen a dead body, his uncle lying in a casket and looking like he'd been removed from himself.

"A Dead One is not the same as a dead thing," his grandmother clarified as if she had read his mind. "A Dead One can move about and even climb trees. It's just that not everyone can see them or wants to see them."

"What makes her dead then?" he asked. It all seemed very confusing. He thought that the dead had to stay still and that was what made them dead.

"It's dying that makes you dead. It's staying still that keeps you that way. A Dead One can't stay still, they need to get up and move around."

Conor thought about this. "Are we all Dead Ones then?"

His grandmother chuckled. "Some could argue . . . But no, Conor, we are very much living. It's just that you have a gift. An ability to see the Dead Ones and talk to them. You can tell them things. You can help their families. Doesn't that sound lovely?"

"Oh no, he isn't doing anything of the sort," his mother finally spoke. "He's not being made a tourist attraction. What happened to Marta, it won't happen to him."

Conor had never heard of a Marta before. He had also never heard his mother speak in such sharp tones, a raggedness to her breath.

His grandmother scowled. "Marta could have done so much more. People need this. It's a gift. It could help so many."

"I don't want you putting that in his head. I brought him here to know. I didn't bring him here for you to give him your duty-and-honor-and-helping speech. I've heard it. If I thought it was a good idea, I could have given it to him myself." His mother stood up and tugged on Conor's arm, forcing him to his feet, the couch released him with reluctance.

"He'll come around to it on his own, anyway. He's a good boy," his grandmother said. "I'll give him the rules, then. Conor, you can listen to the Dead Ones, you can talk to them, but you mustn't ever make them promises. Not ever. Because a Dead One's promise is one that you cannot go back on. And you don't make deals with them neither. A Dead One's deal is never what you think it is. And whatever, whatever, you do, you don't let them take you to the Doctor."

"Oh, the doctor. The girl told me about her!" Conor said, happy to show that he had knowledge.

His grandmother's face changed sharply. Her mouth became tight, eyes widening for a moment. "You don't listen, you don't ever listen, Conor, when they tell you about the Doctor. Do you promise?"

He nodded, there was nothing against him making promises with his grandmother. "Yes, ma'am."

She nodded back and let out a long breath of air. "You remember that promise."

And with those words from his grandmother, his mother hurried him away.

Conor saw Dead Ones off and on after that during his childhood. There was the man with the large hole in his chest stuffed with dog fur and feathers. There was the young, beautiful woman who smiled at Conor in a library once and he had smiled back until he noticed that one of her eyes was a cat's eye marble.

There was the boy he knew, a kid from school, who after disappearing one day on his walk home, appeared to Conor. He was sitting on a park bench, staring at the ground, and Conor had walked up to him. "Dylan?"

Dylan had nodded, not looking up, and Conor had asked. "Everyone's saying you ran away. Are you going home now?"

Dylan had shaken his head, slowly side to side, and Conor had asked, "Why not?"

Dylan raised his head. His eyes were bottle caps and he opened his mouth as if to speak, but his tongue was a skeleton key, glinting within the darkness of his mouth. That was when Conor had stopped being such a happy child.

Conor learned to not approach the Dead Ones because they often tried to engage him in conversation as soon as they realized that he could see them. He learned how to train his gaze so that it could glide past a Dead One without them noticing. They would try to get his attention as he hurried past them, they always wanted things, and so he never listened. He just rushed past, keeping his eyes to the ground, his mouth firmly closed, hands dug deep into his pockets.

Then he turned sixteen and did something foolish. He heard his mother talking on the phone to someone and he heard her say, "What has Marta done now?"

He had not heard the name since all those years before in the house of his grandmother. He watched his mother as she hung up the phone. She looked exhausted, as if the phone conversation had lasted years instead of moments. She turned to him and he asked without thinking the question through, "Who is Marta?"

Maybe his mother wouldn't have answered at any other point, maybe she was caught off guard, maybe she was worn down. "She's my sister."

He felt a jolt go through him. He didn't know that his mother had any siblings. And that her sister, his aunt, could see Dead Ones too. "She is? And she can also see them?"

His mother nodded, defeated by something, life maybe. "Since she was three. She saw a girl walk out of a river. I remember that moment so well. She couldn't stop asking me if I saw the girl, and I didn't. I didn't. Mother knew what was going on, it ran in her family, I guess. I think she wanted to see them too, all along. Jealous of her own daughter, jealous of her own daughter seeing the dead."

"What happened?" Conor asked. "To Marta?"

"She . . . she saw them so much. Mother pushed her to look for them, to do her duty and help people. To spread their messages back to their loved ones. Holy god, who would place that on a child?" Conor realized that his mother wasn't really talking to him so much as talking out loud to herself. She continued, "She started speaking in her sleep, I'd hear her, speaking and speaking and she was always saying 'no.' No. They asked so much of her. She was good and she wanted to help. She wanted so much to help them all. And she said she knew the Doctor would help her if the Doctor could. I never knew what she meant. Mother always said the Doctor was bad. Bad. We found her, you know, we found her when she did it. She was cutting off her hair with a knife. I thought, her hair that isn't so much to lose and then she turned . . ."

"Mom?" he asked. His mother was staring off at some past memory.

"Conor, she had blinded herself." His mother sat down, slumping into a chair. He was glad the chair was there, as she might have crumpled to the ground if it hadn't been.

"Where is she now?"

"A mental institution. Or she was. She died this morning. Swallowed her own tongue. Who can do that to . . . themself?" his mother asked, and Conor wished the words hadn't come out. He knew his mother had needed to speak them, to tell someone, but he wished he could erase the words from the world.

He stared at his mother, not knowing what he could do to help. He went to her and wrapped his arms around her. His mother felt cold. He decided then that there was one Dead One he needed to help.

He went looking for Marta. She was the first Dead One he had ever purposefully sought out. He glanced around the church for her at the funeral. His mother, father, and he were the only people there. His grandmother refused to make an appearance; he wanted to believe that this was out of devastation on her part.

He stared at the coffin, willing Marta to rise from it. She did not. He glanced around the graveyard and he saw the Dead Ones everywhere. Some of them sat on gravestones, some wandered between the rows. One was even kneeling before a gravestone, running her fingers along the engraved name on it and crying. He had never seen a Dead One crying. She looked so completely alive in her grief.

He did not see Marta. His mother leaned against his father. He looked at them and wondered how they had fallen in love. It seemed such a strange question never to have considered before. He wondered if it was something that happened fast or if it was gradual. He wondered if the Dead Ones saw his parents and longed for something so simple as the ability to lean their heads against the shoulder of someone who loved them.

They left the graveyard and he looked about as they walked away. Marta was still not anywhere to be seen. Conor tried to imagine the places she might turn up. He had never known her and so he had no idea which places she might choose to haunt: had there been a spot in the city that she loved? Did anywhere hold memories for her? Was there a place where she had had a first kiss? A playground that she had loved as a child? A certain section of stacks in the library where she hid as a teenager devouring books? Or was there nothing? Had she always been cursed by sight and so had never felt connected to anywhere?

Conor spent weeks looking for her. He didn't find her. And so he did something even more foolish. He went looking for the Doctor.

She was easier to find. He knew that all the Dead Ones knew her. He saw a Dead One leaning against the outside of a building. She was in her twenties, or she had been in her twenties and now would always be in her twenties, and had long red hair. She was pretty in the sort of way that some girls can be only at certain moments in their lives—rebelling against something and wearing that rebellion like a second skin. He went up to her. He knew she was a Dead One because of her arms, the cuts along the veins patched over with Lisa Frank stickers.

"Excuse me," he said to her.

She looked up at him, startled that he could see her. "Hey, shit, you can, whoa."

He nodded. "I can see you, yes."

"How?" She peered at him, closely, as if she could see the ability on his skin, as if he might be wearing a badge that said *I see dead people. Ask me my name!*

He shrugged. "Just can. I need to ask you something."

"That seems like a fucked-up reversal. Aren't we supposed to be asking you for something? To pass on messages or sing down some stones and lead us out of this hell or your immortal soul or something?" she said. She crossed her arms over her chest, playing at defiance, but Conor knew that she was trying to hide her sticker-covered veins from view.

"It is what is. I need to find the Doctor."

The girl stared at him, her mouth opened slightly. She blinked a few times.

"Please," he added.

"The Doctor? You want to meet her? Why?"

"She's the only one who can help me find someone. It's important."

The girl thought about it. "Okay, fine, I could help you. But you'd have to make me a deal."

Conor gulped. He had expected as much, but it still made his stomach drop like he was on a quickly descending elevator. "What kind of deal?"

"I want you to get the Doctor to talk to me. She won't talk to us."

The deal seemed straightforward enough. Conor wondered what traps could lie within it. "Okay."

"Do you promise?" the girl asked. Her voice had risen a notch, she sounded younger.

He wondered if he shouldn't just run now, but he remembered his mother, sitting in her warm room and still feeling so chilled. "I promise."

The girl nodded and started to walk away. "Follow me then. I'm Alicia, by the by. What's your name?"

"Conor."

She smiled. "I heard a story about a Conor once, or maybe that wasn't his name. It was something Irish-sounding."

"What was the story?" he asked as he began to follow her.

"Well, he was real drunk at the pub at closing time. As the Irish are known for and whatnot. He's walking home and he, because he's drunk, he forgets that you aren't supposed to walk through the graveyard at midnight. So he does.

"And he's walking and he hears this voice calling his name. 'Conor! Conor!' but he can't see nobody around. And then he feels this weight on his back all of a sudden, and it's a heavy weight.

"And he's scared, he's trying to shake it off of him, whatever it is, but he can't. And then he realizes that it's a fuckin' body on his back, its arms are wrapped around his shoulders. And he starts screaming as, you know, anyone would rightfully do in the situation." She stopped speaking for a moment, and Conor looked up, startled, to find that it had become evening around them although he had been sure it had only been three o'clock when he had first walked up to the girl. He looked around them and he didn't recognize the surroundings anymore. They were in front of a deep, dark wood.

"Then the voice speaks to him," she continued. "'You found my body, Conor O'Fain, and now you must take me to my burial ground.' 'But we were just at the cemetery,' Conor said, and his voice was pleading. 'They won't let me be buried there, but there's a cemetery only a few miles from here and they will take me.' And Conor is terrified. He's freaking out. But he knows the cemetery that the body speaks of and so he begins to walk in that direction."

They stepped into the woods, Conor close behind Alicia, afraid to let her out of his sight.

"And all the time the body is talking to him and telling him to hurry. And finally Conor says, 'What's the big rush? You're already dead. Don't you have all the time in the world?' And the voice says, 'Well, I do but you don't. If you don't get rid of me by sunup, then you'll have to carry me forever.' And Conor starts running, but the body is heavy and the road is uneven, and it is hard to run on."

Conor didn't look around himself. He could sense there was something wrong about the trees in the forest, but he didn't want to know what it was. He kept his eyes on Alicia's back.

"And so finally the sun is starting to rise. Those red fingers of dawn are stretching out and tickling away the stars. And he is running, but he sees the gates of the graveyard and he races through them. He made it! He made it! And the voice says, 'You've made it. I didn't believe you could do it, but you've made it' and the body drops from his shoulders to the ground. And Conor is thinking that he shouldn't look at the body, he shouldn't see its face, but he just can't help himself. No one ever can in stories, can they? And he looks down and the body is him." Alicia stopped speaking and stopped walking. Conor nearly walked into her. In front of them was a tiny cottage that looked like it belonged in another century.

"We're here," Alicia said.

"But is the story over?" Conor asked. Alicia nodded, and so he asked, "But what the hell does it mean?"

She shrugged. "Does anyone ever know?"

He stared at the door of the cottage. It was rounded and had colored glass windows in the center. "Should I knock?"

Alicia nodded again, and so he went up to the door and knocked. It swung open. He took one last look at Alicia, who looked less rebellious. She looked like a confused teenager who had seen something horrible and didn't know how to respond except to stop caring. He stepped inside the cottage. The door swung shut behind him.

The cottage smelled of buttermilk pancakes cooking on a griddle and of spiced apple cider. He walked toward the kitchen and peeked inside. The Doctor sat at a wooden table. She was looking down at something and all he could see of her was her dark hair hanging around her face. He didn't want to startle her, "Hello?"

She didn't speak or look up, but she motioned for him to take the seat across from her. He did. He looked at her. She was young, though he wouldn't have been able to pin her age except to say she was between fifteen and thirty-five. She had creamy skin, and her eyes were wide and dark. "Hello, Conor."

"Hello, miss, er, Doctor," he said.

"I am the Doctor. You have come to the correct destination. How can I help you?"

"Well, it's about my aunt."

"You have two aunts that I have known."

"My aunt Marta, the one who was like me. Who could see the Dead Ones."

The doctor frowned. "The Dead Ones?"

"Yeah, the Dead Ones. The ghosts or whatever."

"Oh, the dead, yes. Marta could see them. I remember how she asked me why she had such a power. I didn't know how to answer. I said that maybe she was just looking more closely than anyone else was."

Conor shifted in his seat. The Doctor had a soft yet deep voice. She sounded like he imagined fairy godmothers sounded in fairy tales. "And what did you do to her?"

The Doctor looked down, again. "I didn't heal her. I couldn't. I can't heal the living. I've tried, you know, that was the deal I had made. That I could heal the living, but I guess in deals you have to be more specific with your words, don't you? Because I can heal their sickness and their wounds, but I can't fix everything. I can't stop how painful it all is. Blessed, they called me. The blessed child. And here I am with all of my cures, and none that mean anything."

"The Dead Ones, the dead, they say you heal them, but you do it so badly. Leaves for hands? Bottle caps for eyes? What is that supposed to help?" Conor felt an anger welling up inside him. He didn't know that it had been lurking inside of him all of that time. He remembered a little boy with a key.

The Doctor's hands were shaking. "I'm not supposed to, that wasn't part of the deal. I have no cures for them, and so I have to work with what I can beg, borrow, or steal. I'm not supposed to, but how can I not? They all have such ache in them."

"And what about Marta? Is she here and healed by you?"

The Doctor sighed. "She is. She didn't want me to restore her sight, but she wanted her voice."

Someone walked through the doorway. Conor knew it was his aunt. She looked like a younger version of his mother, but faded out like a Polaroid snapped and left in the sun. Her hair was white and she wore a blindfold across her eyes. A raven sat on her shoulder. She walked over to him, passing the Doctor, and letting one hand brush over the hand of the Doctor. She opened her mouth and the raven did as well, mimicking the movements she made. He realized as she began to speak that it was the raven who was talking. "Don't blame her, Conor. She's as lost as us, you know. It's not fair. It's never been fair. It'll never be fair. I learned that eventually. You can't do everything, you can't save everyone. You just try to help where you can."

"My mom, your sister, she," and his voice broke. He didn't know how to explain.

Marta shushed him, she walked over to him and whispered in his ear. She told him a story. It wasn't a long story, but it was a good story. When the story was done, she walked back out of the room.

Conor looked up at the Doctor and she looked at him. "Is there anything else you need of me?"

He nodded. "There was a girl who showed me here. Alicia. She wanted to ask you something. She said you wouldn't talk to them, the dead."

The Doctor shook her head. "I can't talk to them. It's my punishment for healing them. I lose them. I can't even see them once I've healed them."

"But, Marta was just here. You saw her."

The Doctor shook her head. "Oh, especially not her. I can never see her." She smiled faintly at some memory. "And what does Alicia wish of me? Go ask her, and I shall grant it if I can."

He went out to Alicia and asked her what she wanted. Then he returned to the Doctor. "She'd like something other than stickers. She says they make her feel childish."

The Doctor stood up and walked to the shelves that lined the walls of the kitchen. She pulled out two scarves and handed them to him. "Tie them tight for her."

He nodded. "Thanks."

"My pleasure, Conor."

He left and went to Alicia and helped her tie the scarves over her wounds. "I like the color. It suits you."

She smiled, and her smile was radiant, it was life. He and Alicia walked out of the woods, and as he stepped from the trees he was back in his city and it was day again. He looked around, but Alicia was gone. Conor walked home.

He found his mother in the kitchen, she was making soup and the smell of tomatoes and garlic filled the air. He went up to her and hugged her. She laughed, "What's that for?"

"When you were little and your sister was even littler, you'd build snow forts, and the two of you would climb inside and it would be warm because the snow shielded you and you'd tell stories to Marta. And she said that was the happiest she ever was, that she never felt safer than hidden in the snow with you near her. And she misses you and she loves you and she wants you to know that you gave her happiness."

His mother stared at him. She stared at him for the longest time. And then, though there were tears in her eyes, his mother smiled. Conor smiled back, but his body felt heavy under his skin.

CONOR LAID THE CARDS OUT one by one. He looked behind the woman for a second and then he picked up three of the cards. "And there were three who got lost."

He tore the three cards into pieces. The woman gasped and held a hand against her mouth. He threw the pieces into the air. "And the ones left behind. They thought that they were lost forever."

The woman watched the pieces fall to the ground. He scooped up the remaining cards and handed the woman the deck. "Shuffle them."

She did, though her hands were trembling.

He took the deck back and began to lay down the cards. One-by-one he went through the deck, until there were only three cards remaining. He laid them down and saw that they were the cards he had just thrown away. The woman pulled in her breath, sharply.

"But they never left, you know. They are always there. Because you're there, and you remember them and sometimes that's enough."

The woman began to sob, some release shaking itself free from her body. He looked behind her again at the three who stood behind her. They nodded at him in thanks. He nodded back, and even that weight of movement was so heavy to his exhausted body. He knew he was doing what he could, because that was the thing with deals, you did with them what you could.

# Long in the Tooth

THE LESSON IS OBVIOUS. THERE will always be wolves in the woods. The woods will always be deep and dark. Anyone who strays from the path will always be punished. No matter that the forest floor was flooded with moss, so deep and green, so soft beneath the feet. No matter that there were flowers that only grew in the shade, such delicate buds. No matter how easy it was to follow the song of a bird without realizing. No matter that paths are not always easy to keep oneself upon.

The lesson is as old as time.

If you meet a wolf, he will always try to trick you. His teeth can only be sharp. His growl is one that is meant to get caught in the throat. It sounds like thunder if you listen closely. And you count and you count before you remember that thunder follows lightning and not the other way around. You are waiting for disaster and it's already come. What are you counting until?

The lesson is simple.

You taught the ones you love to keep themselves safe without telling them that's what you were doing. You'd glance from side to side when crossing a street, hurry your feet when going past shadows, tell no one your whole name at first. Such simple things to learn, our calculations of what we must do to survive. No one told you how all those additions, these things to remember, could also feel like subtractions. How the wolf might still be waiting—a multiplication of time and distance and fear. How the division at the center of the lesson was always going to equal yourself.

The lesson is universal.

The wolf is always a wolf. The wolf sharpens his claws every day with every step. Sometimes the wolf is a tiger. Sometimes the tiger is a hyena. Sometimes the hyena is a monster, creeping out of a cave. A castle. The lake behind the house. The wolf is everything and nothing. The claws are so sharp. The teeth are so quick. Sometimes even you are the wolf. You don't realize it until you're old. You see it in the mirror, the way you shift and pace, like an animal caged. How much the running you have wanted is screaming under your skin, in your bones. Your claws are no longer sharp. You've spent so much time in the shadows cast by staying in the light.

The lesson is empty.

You walk in the woods, slip free from the path. The smell of the earth greets you after the rain. The woods are so deep and so dark, and so easy to fall inside of. Was there ever a path to begin with? You can't find it now. It's all just moss beds and twisting roots and the flitter of bird wings and the rush of feet scurry scurrying. You could stop for a rest. You could wait for a traveler. You can taste it almost. All that you leave behind. There will always be wolves in the woods. You know this. You've found them, after all.

# Even the Veins of Leaves

IT ALWAYS SEEMS LIKE WINTER comes earlier along the stretch of road that winds between the forest—at some point there must have been a good reason to slice through the vast acreage of trees and make a road, though now there are ways to go around it, keep on the highway, avoid the forest path. Maybe the shade from the tree cover is the reason for that extra bit of chill. That sounds scientific and like it just could be right.

I grew up not far from the forest, but I never saw much reason for going near it. Parents liked to scare their children, keep them away from the trees with ghost stories. But, in reality, there were a lot of poachers who set up traps inside the woods, and there was always a chance of getting clamped into one. A boy, a few years older than me, had it happen to him. Larry Fields—that was his name. He went in on some dare among his group of nitwit friends to see who would go the deepest into the woods, and now he's got one leg that ends at the knee.

It's one of the largest forests on the continent. I looked that up once, unable to believe that it wasn't the largest, but it isn't. To me, it had always seemed like it went on forever. Lovely, dark, and deep, and all that. Though I'd have never called it lovely, to be fair. Awesome maybe, in the original meaning of the word. I was filled with a sort of near-terror at the vastness of the trees.

THE CALL CAME IN ON a Monday morning. A couple of kids missing on a hike in the forest. Normally, that wouldn't have been my department. Leave it to the Rangers and all. But my partner wanted to help. There had been some animosity between the sheriff's department and the Park Service Rangers. This was a way to put out the flames on the bridge.

We parked the patrol vehicle near the spot where the teens' car was found. We knew at least where it was probable that they had entered the forest. That was more of a lead than a lot of searches got.

It was Ranger Stevens working the search. Just he and a trainee whom I'd never met. He nodded to me and my partner, Wilkins.

"Scott, Avery." Stevens greeted us with a nod. He didn't bother to introduce the trainee. He probably didn't want to waste head space learning names when he could be cataloguing trees.

"Deputies," the trainee said. I was young and the trainee looked younger. The age discrepancy between us was obvious.

"So I assume we got no dings off their phone GPS?" Wilkins asked, one hand unconsciously going to his own pocket to tap his phone. Wilkins, I was sure, would have trouble existing without a phone signal. It always surprised me that he didn't head toward a bigger city. He wasn't incompetent as a cop, so he could've found work in a place that agreed with him more.

Stevens laughed. "You know how it is. You come within a mile of this forest and your phone might as well be one of those rotary deals." He held up his walkie-talkie as he said, "We're on the Talkies from here on out."

"What's the info we got on the kids?" I asked, looking into the forest. I had a clear view of about ten yards and after that the leaves and undergrowth swallowed up my vision's path.

"Three teens, two sixteen and one seventeen. All males. They went in yesterday, according to their folks."

"Just hiking? Or they have a set destination?" Wilkins asked.

"Just hiking, from what their parents knew," Stevens said. Wilkes and Stevens moved quickly ahead, as if hoping to give me space to talk to the trainee. They never knew what to do with anyone younger than themselves.

"Are there any destinations around here?" the trainee asked, turning to me.

I held in a laugh. The phrase hadn't been intended to be funny I was sure, but the way the trainee phrased the question made it sound like he wasn't just asking about the forest, but the whole county. "There's a couple 'famous' trees around-abouts, but nothing of a real particular pull for teenagers." Then, feeling sorry for him, I introduced myself. "I'm Avery Morgan, by the way. You are?"

He nodded at me, acknowledging the answer, and I could see that he was holding back a laugh as well, probably at the idea of famous trees. "Lukas."

We headed into the forest. There were seven hours of light remaining, though only six hours of it would be actual good light. The chances of finding the kids in a preliminary search weren't great.

But the weather was still good, not yet into full fall, when the nights fell quickly below freezing, and there was no rain in the forecast. There was no need to panic about the safety of the teens. Not yet.

There weren't many missing people who weren't found. Not really, when you thought about the size of the forest and the rising number of hikers, campers, what-have-yous in the past twenty or so years. I remembered a little girl when I was around ten or so. Her family had been camping, and she wandered off. She was an unfound. And there was a young couple a few years back, right before I joined the sheriff's department. They were in their twenties. The woman had curly blonde hair and the man had a scar through one of his eyebrows. They were hiking in the photo that the newspapers ran—both staring at the camera, the woman caught in mid-laugh. The photo had that quality of seeming like it came from someone's past. I never had a sense of someone being dead before just from seeing a photograph, but I did with that one. There was something about them caught in that moment of happiness that made them seem like they were trapped in that moment of time. Years later, and they were never found, not even the bodies.

"How long you been with the sheriff's office?" Lukas had matched my gait, walking beside me in the lead.

"Three and a half years. You just join the Park Service?" I checked around us every so often, glancing to the sides for signs of someone moving off the sort-of path that we were on. These could be found all over the forests: some from hikers who liked to set off on the same path to avoid just the thing that had probably happened to the teens—getting off track and unable to determine which way led you back, some from deer following the same safe routes every day and trampling the undergrowth down.

"Yeah . . . Well, I mean really just. I just got into town. And then get called out. I guess it's a good way to train, get tossed right into the fire." Lukas must have been a talker, because there was a certain lack of pausing in his flow of words, as if he were completely comfortable making conversation anywhere, with anyone.

"Ah, yeah," I said. I had an equal skill for shutting down conversations anywhere, with anyone. I sped up my walk incrementally, not enough to appear rude, but enough that Lukas would have to rush in order to keep up. It was one of the life-long pleasures of long legs: getting away from any situation without breaking a sweat.

"Avery!' Wilkins said it sharply. I spun, expecting him to be glaring at my speed-walking. Wilkins seemed to live a life where speed didn't exist. But he wasn't glaring at me. He was staring at something off the path. I jogged back to him and he pointed toward something in the trees. I turned to stare.

There was a young man, probably one of the sixteen-year-olds, sitting at the base of a tree. His back was pressed against the trunk, and his head hung. I stepped off the path and towards him.

"Hello?" I ventured, having forgotten the teens' names already, if I had known them to begin with. I unconsciously tugged on the cord hanging around my neck. It was a charm of sorts, an old habit I'd never been able to break.

The boy did not look up. His chest appeared to be moving, he was breathing, and he looked uninjured. "Hello?"

I took a couple of steps closer. The boy moved, just a little, a certain shudder of the shoulders. He was crying, silently, trying to hold in any sound. I reached out and touched his shoulder. My fingertips just grazed the fabric of his shirt and he screamed. The sound made me take a startled step backward, nearly tripping over a rock behind me.

Wilkins caught me. He pushed in front and toward the boy. "Son?" Wilkins was using his Dad-voice. I'd heard it before, when he was talking to his kids, but I'd never heard how comforting it sounded until that moment.

"P—p-p-p-lease. Pl-pl-ease," the boy was muttering. His voice shaking and quavering. "I'm, I'm s-s-sorry. I don't want to see."

"There's no need to be sorry. We're here now, from the Sheriff's Department. I'm Deputy Wilkins. That's Deputy Morgan, who was talking to you a moment ago. Are you hurt?"

The boy kept crying, but he also nodded his head. Wilkins reached out as if to comfort the boy. Stevens and Lukas stood behind me, I hadn't heard them approaching. We all must have collectively been holding our breaths. Wilkins hand reached the boy's shoulder just as the boy looked up.

"Fuck me," Stevens said, the words coming out as a gasp.

The boy's eyes were tightly shut, and there was blood streaking down from beneath his lids mixed in with the tears.

○

"He's lucky, actually. He's going to keep his eyes, with only a little corneal damage. Something scratched that boy's eyes pretty damn bad," Doctor Andover said. He was the town's main doctor and had been for years. I was surprised to see him working the ER shift. He had narrowed his eyes at me and muttered something about everyone needing to do their turn.

"What scratched him?" I asked. "Tree branches?"

Doctor Andover sighed audibly. "Tree branches, Avery? You think tree branches scratched that boy's eyes without damaging any other part of his face?"

"Just offering a suggestion, doc."

"An incredibly helpful one, too," Andover said, cracking his neck by bending it side to side. "What I'd guess, though don't hold me to it, is that he scratched his own eyes. There was blood under his fingernails, and he'd have had the precision to do it."

"The precision to do it? What about the want? I mean, who scratches their own eyes?"

Doctor Andover nearly rolled his eyes. "Avery, you seemed so bright as a child, yet as an adult I'm finding you disappointing in terms of intelligence." He paused before continuing, as if he was waiting for me to catch up. "Three teenage boys wander into the woods and get lost. Do you think, maybe, they were on something? Drugs create an improbability in people's actions. An improbability that we can make a probability in improbable situations. My guess is these boys were blitzed out on something, got lost, and then freaked out."

I decided not to pursue it. "Did he say anything that'll help us find the other two? Where they were heading or anything?"

"Nothing that made sense. I've given him a mild sedative, so he'll be asleep for a while. He said something about a town. A town in the forest. So I'm not sure that even awake he'll be any help."

A town. I didn't let Andover see it, but I felt something on my skin. As if the air in the room had dropped in temperature and a shiver was running across my flesh. There was a local legend. One I'd heard bits and pieces of as a kid. It was about a town that tried to start in the forest at one point, before the road, before our own town, before anything really. A town where everyone had disappeared, gobbled up by something in the forest, and then the town itself was overgrown. Sometimes, according to the tall tales, something would come out of the town, trying to find a way out of the forest. No one ever said what that something was. Of course that made the story much more frightening. "Thanks, doc."

Leaving the hospital, I noticed a middle-aged couple who I guessed were the boy's parents. Sheriff Oliver was talking to them, and he tipped his head once to me in brief acknowledgment as I went past. The mother was tugging at the bottom of her sweater, as if trying to pull it down over her body, to cover herself entirely. The father was nodding methodically, dazed, nodding even when Oliver seemed to not have said anything at all.

"Ave, what's up? You're more catatonic than usual even," my sister, Lena, said. She had called me. A weekly check-in that I both appreciated and wondered about. I heard her youngest child in the background, yelling for a baba.

"Just got three kids missing in the forest. Well, two, we found one."

"Alive?" she asked.

I went to the cupboard and pulled out a can of tomatoes, opened it, and then dumped them into a sauce pan. Adding olive oil, I said, "Yeah, he was messed up, though. Not getting a lot out that'll help us find the others."

"Jeez, that sucks. How long they been missing?"

I stirred in some basil, started to chop some cloves of garlic. "Just a day, two days tomorrow. Lena?"

"Yeah?"

"Do you remember a story about a town in the forest?"

There was a long pause from Lena. I added the garlic to the sauce, stirred it, and adjusted the temperature. Finally, she spoke, "I think so. The story that always used to freak you out, right?"

"I don't know if I'd say that . . ." I began.

She interrupted, "Yeah, yeah, don't you remember? Cousin Francie would tell it to us, and you'd cover your ears and pretend to sing. Like *la la la*. You know?"

"Maybe. Yeah, maybe." I set a second pot onto the stove, filled with water to boil. "What was the story, do you remember?"

"No, sorry, no. That was years ago. I just remember how much it scared you, I guess. I think I smacked Francie because she wouldn't stop telling it, just to mess with you." The baby got loud in the background again. "I gotta let you go, Ave. Hope you find those kids."

"Me too. Night, Lena."

"Night," she said, ending the call just in time to cut off a particularly loud wail of *baba*.

I finished making supper, sat down at the table, ate a couple of bites, then let the rest cool too much to be enjoyable.

WE WERE BACK IN THE woods. There were more people from the sheriff's office, as well as the Park Service this time, and we also had a plan. We'd circle out from the point we found the boy at in widening gyres. Maps were brought out and radio frequencies synched, and we were each assigned a "buddy." One ranger to one cop. I of course ended up with Lukas. This was the sort of thing that always happened, youngest goes with youngest, even if they did it unconsciously. I always wanted things to be done by quietest goes with quietest, but I didn't make the plans.

"So they said the boy isn't going to lose his eyesight. That's good," Lukas said.

"Yeah," I responded, unable to use my outpacing trick since the buddy-system of a SAR didn't really work if you were purposefully trying to lose your buddy.

"I heard drugs, maybe, were involved?"

"I don't think the drug screen is back yet. Don't wanna go making assumptions."

"Oh, no, of course not. I was just . . ." he let his words trail off. We walked in silence for a while.

I didn't know all the trees. Not by name anyway, though I had seen most of them at some point or another. Always had meant to take a course in dendrology or something like that, but I never went into the forests enough to think it was necessary.

The trees around us were mostly conifers, and there were some needles on the ground, already gone to shades of brown. They crunched as we walked over them.

"Dendrophobia," Lukas said from behind me. I wasn't sure if it was an out-of-nowhere interjection or if he'd been talking for a while with me not paying attention.

"Huh?"

"That's what they call a fear of trees or forests," he said. Then perhaps taking note of my look of confusion, "Sorry, I'd been trying to remember, and it finally came to me."

"You afraid of trees?"

"No, though it would be funny if I was and joined the Park Service, right?" he said, grinning. "I knew a girl who was, though. Terrified of trees, especially at night. I guess when she was a kid her family went camping a lot and one time she got lost. Not even in a big wood, but she was little and so any size was huge, you know? I've never really liked trees though. Something about them irritates me."

I nodded. I figured a verbal response was akin to encouragement to him. He was about to speak, again, I could hear him taking in a breath, when the sound came. It was a sharp snap, like someone taking a large twig and breaking it in half over their knee. Too loud and purposeful sounding to be an animal walking nearby. I looked at Lukas, holding a finger over my lips, and cocked my head to the side that I thought the sound had come from. There was a snapping again, but it didn't sound quite right. Not like wood exactly. It sounded like bones. My father collected bones he found in the woods, with some plan of making them into artwork of some kind. I remembered he showed me the rib cage of a deer. Perfectly cleaned, white, pristine. I'd recently broken my leg falling from a tree, and I was fascinated by bones and the fact that something inside the body could snap. So my father let me try to break the rib cage. I tried with my hands, just bending the bone as hard as I could, but that didn't work. Then my father tried and he couldn't do it either. Finally we used a hammer. And I still remembered the sound of the bones breaking and wondering why I hadn't been able to hear my own bone breaking. I couldn't sleep that night, nauseous feeling.

The snapping sound was almost exactly the same as the sound of that deer rib breaking. Lukas looked at me and whispered, "That doesn't sound like a tree branch, does it?"

I shook my head.

Snap.

That time it sounded closer.

"Jesus . . ." Lukas muttered.

I gave him a sharp glance, hoping he'd get the clue and shut up. The snapping stopped. Everything was silent. In fact, it was too quiet: no birds, no hum of insects, no rustling of tree leaves. It was like we were in a vacuum. The wind was gone.

Up ahead, something shimmered, like when you held up a mirror and bounced the light off it. A friend and I used to do that; kids trying out things we'd seen on TV. The light was shimmering up, up, up. It fell upon me, and I saw the dance of light on my hand. My skin looked strange lit up like that, younger maybe. I went toward where the light came from.

"Avery?" Lukas' voice behind me, concerned and questioning.

Faster. Faster. Running through the woods, I smashed into something that I hadn't even noticed in front of me. Warmth dripped down my face. What the hell was in front of me?

It was a house. I'd run into the closed door of a house. This was protected land. There should have been no house here. Looking at it, it was an old house. Like colonial times or earlier old.

"What the fuck . . ." I said out loud. The words broke the unnatural hush, and then I was back. Reaching up, I rubbed off the wet on my face. My hand was covered in blood, nose felt broken or at least well smashed. Stepping back, I took in the entirety of the house. It was tiny and covered in overgrowth. I spun around, there were other houses. They were close together.

I'd heard about this before. Ghost villages had been found in places that were never have thought to be settled. But not this forest, other than of course in the legends.

"Hey, Lukas!" I shouted. Feeling dizzy and hoping he'd appear, but more than to help me. I just wanted to show off the strangeness of what I'd found.

He came running through the woods. "Whoa, Avery, shit. Your face."

I touched my face again. The blood was so warm.

The trees were taller here. How deep in the woods were we?

"I ran into the house," I said.

He frowned. "House?"

"The houses, they're overgrown, but they're houses," I said, pointing to the one that had smashed up my face.

Lukas looked in the right direction but there was no wave of understanding that rushed over his face. "I think you hit yourself a little too hard there. Why don't you let me take you back to the others?"

He was standing in front of a white-skinned tree, so tall. And the sunlight filtered down through the leaves and Lukas seemed to shimmer for an instant. There was no shadow. That's what was wrong. The trees had long shadows.

And Lukas didn't.

I nodded at him. All those stories about something wanting to get out of the forest. What if it had already found a way out and wanted to bring people back in?

When my father had given me the shard of the broken deer bone, I'd kept it. It was supposed to be a reminder of the fragility of the human body. I had taken it as something else, a charm of sorts. When I entered the police, I'd carved the shard into something sharp, wore it around my neck like a talisman. I put one hand up to cord that held it around my neck, made to look as if I was massaging the muscle.

Lukas smiled, beckoning. I made to follow him, just needed to get my bearings. I could run fast.

"So why'd you ever leave?" I asked.

"Leave?" he asked. We were walking away from the houses, the darkness of their insides I could glimpse from where there once were windows, empty eyes.

"The woods," I replied.

He chuckled. "You're smarter than a smalltown cop, Avery. I've met a few of you, you know. The woods have many borders and I've been here for a long, long time."

"What are you?"

He laughed harder. "You know how tall some trees get and how deep those roots must go and how far they must spread out? Do you know what those roots disturb, cracking through the earth?"

I felt dizzy. The blood was caking my shirt, drying the cloth into brittleness. How much blood had I lost? I felt nauseous. "What are you?"

He shook his head. He was slowing his pace, coming to the end of wherever we were going. I saw a path to the side, a deer path probably. I pulled on the cord around my neck, one sharp yank and the shard was in my hand.

"Avery, you get a choice, you know. I always give that. Do you want to see before?"

"See what?" I asked.

"How deep the woods really are?" he said, turning to me. A smile spread across his face, eyes bright. I slammed the shard of bone into his eye and he screamed. His scream was the sound of the wind roaring.

I started to run, not looking back, never looking back. The trees seemed to move out of my way, swaying with the breeze as if to show me a path. My legs felt like they were being cut from the inside, my lungs were on fire. I ran.

I burst from the trees and onto the road. That cold, cold stretch. The police vehicles were parked there. I saw Wilkins and he saw me, his expression changing from one of surprise at me bursting out from the trees to worry in an instant. "Avery, what in the name—"

"It's Lukas, Lukas," I babbled, before collapsing.

LATER, IN THE HOSPITAL, AFTER x-rays and pain killers and sleep, when I could talk sense, Wilkins questioned me.

"You said something about a Lukas, Avery? When you came out of the woods?"

"The trainee park ranger. The one I was teamed with."

"Hell, Avery, you weren't paired with anyone. I know you never listen to SAR procedure, so I didn't pair you up. The doctor said your head was alright, yeah?"

I stared at him. Finally I said, "There's a town in the forest."

He shook his head. "That's what the kids are always saying. Did you hear that story growing up too?"

I shrugged.

"They even told it when I was a kid. A town was made and the trees didn't like it. So they started growing, blocking it in. But the town was angry, hated those trees. The trees won, I think. Maybe. I don't quite remember."

"I hope they do," I said.

Wilkins looked at me for a moment. "Get some sleep, kid."

○

OCCASIONALLY, NOW AND only when I have to, I drive past the forest on my way to somewhere else. I've noticed how the trees are succumbing to disease, first the birches and now the other species. I wonder if, in years and years, the trees will mostly be gone. What then will become of us if the forest's secrets are finally left in the open for everyone to see?

# Run the Line

ALL THE FOOTBALL PLAYERS GLORY knows are dead, but they still show up for games. Her brother was the running back of the high school team, and when the school bus bringing them home from an away game two years before hit a spot of black ice, the bus swerved and slid and lost control, and the team must have shouted, and then there was nothing. It must have been so cold in the water. Glory thinks about this more than she should, though less than she could.

Glory doesn't really know much about football, though she always watched her brother's games and still does. They called him Lightning Luke. He was so fast, so graceful that he could spin and swerve around the opposing team's players as if they weren't even there. If the bus had been Luke, then everyone would have survived.

His best friend was the quarterback, Tom. Tom was tall, and off the field he spoke so quietly that people had trouble hearing him. But Luke always heard him, would repeat what Tom said just a little louder so everyone could hear. He'd say, "Oh, Tom, that's an interesting point about how Hester acts like the ghost and the whole town is haunted," and everyone in class would nod and understand that Tom had said something deep and thoughtful and Luke was just the conduit. Glory thinks they must have been sitting next to each other on the bus. That was something, even if it wasn't much.

On Homecoming, everyone at the school knows the team will come back. It's tradition. People don't miss games, especially not big ones. The school hasn't had to have tryouts in the years since the bus accident. Glory never gets to talk to her brother on game days; no one does. But the other teams' players still taunt them, try to get them to mess up. They're never too cruel though; they never bring up that all the boys are dead, will never come back, will never get to drink hot cocoa after the game, never kiss someone just because they won. Instead, they say, you suck, your mama could play better.

Glory is now the same age as her older brother. It is the math of tragedies. He used to call her kiddo, would throw Beanie Babies at her when she wasn't looking, would take her on drives with him at night to get ice cream. He'd say, "One day all of this will be yours" and point at the hand-me-down car from their parents.

On the night of the big game, she goes early to get a bleacher seat nearest to the field. She sits next to Cassie, the girlfriend of one of the defensive linemen. She hasn't dated anyone since, says maybe she will when she's in college because here it feels like he was still around. The weather is sharp and cool, but not yet cold enough to shiver. Except when the team enters the field and the air temp always drops for a moment, and Glory can see her breath.

When she was little, she liked building snow forts and hiding inside them. She'd watch her breath melt the edges. Luke would peek in the doorway and throw cookies at her, pieces of candy, he'd ask her how her Arctic mission was going.

When the team enters the field, they look out at the stands but never make eye contact with anyone. Glory is not sure if they do it on purpose or if it's something else, if they are kept from it by some rule of the dead. She wonders if they see everybody, the whole town practically, bundled in warm coats, and ready to cheer for their team.

The game stretches through the night. Every touchdown is traded off with the opposing team. The crowd leans forward as one, every single body tensed. They are ready for victory.

A week or two before the accident, they drove for ice cream and Luke talked about college. He said, "Do you think I'll have to play football there too?" Glory had been surprised hearing him, she'd always thought he'd loved the game. Lightning Luke. "You don't have to do anything," she'd said. She had imagined a life spinning out for her brother, maybe he'd be an artist or a cook or an engineer. Maybe he'd fly to space, or dive into the ocean to look for endangered octopuses. He'd smiled at her, "Maybe I won't, then." As if it was as easy as that since she'd said it. As if he'd never had such a thought before.

On the field, Luke is running with the ball. He is dodging and dancing around the opposition. Glory wants to shout that he can drop it if he wants. But she never yells. She sometimes sits out in the cold until ice forms on her eyelashes. But she never yells.

It's a touchdown and the crowd goes wild. They chant his name. Lightning Luke. Lightning Luke. He was seventeen. They'd all always be seventeen. Always be football uniforms and nicknames. Glory wants to explore the world for him, to eat every dish and touch every tree. She will come home every year until he looks at the crowd and sees her.

Lightning Luke. Lightning. Luke. For once, she chants it, too. It might as well be a prayer.

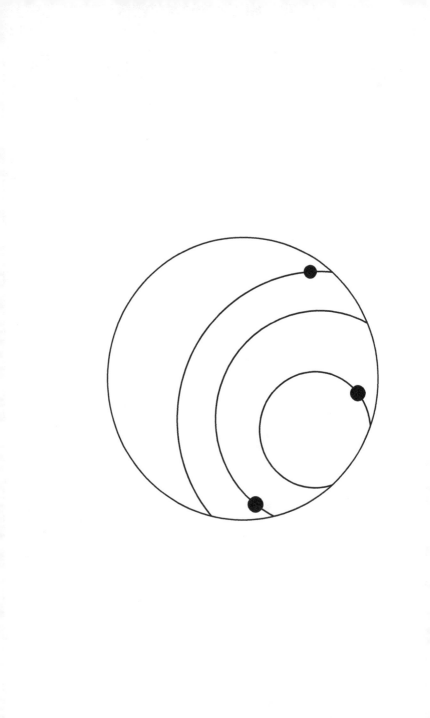

# Accidental Girls

WHEN I SEE HALLEY IN A bar, years and years past when she disappeared, I know it's her so quickly and completely that it makes me gasp. The Halley of her thirties is leaner than her teenage self, her hair dyed a blue so dark that in the shady bar I think it's black, and she has a scar across one cheek. But she still has eyes the color of rainy days, a slight limp on her left side. I wonder if she also has a face etched with living, laugh lines around her eyes, a frown line permanently drawn across her forehead.

"Halley?" I half-shout across the bar. But she doesn't even flinch or turn. I move through the other bar patrons as quickly as I can, trying not to lose her in the crowd. When I catch up to her she's talking to a man in jeans and a band shirt of some musician I've never heard of. I reach out and tap her shoulder.

She flinches. The man stares at me and she turns. We haven't been face-to-face since we were sixteen, sitting in my front yard, drinking lemonade in paper cups, talking about what senior year would be like. That was the day before she went missing. The day before everything slipped and crashed. "Do I know you?" she asks.

"It's Abby?" For a second I feel like maybe I'm the one in the wrong. That she's still Halley but I'm someone else.

She shakes her head. "I'm sorry? I don't think I know you?"

"From school? Lincoln. We were friends." Friends feels incomplete.

She half-smiles. "I really don't think I know you. I'm not sure what Lincoln is. I get confused for others all the time."

"You're not Halley Blackwell?"

She shakes her head. But her face is Halley's face, and her head shake, always so confident and yet so disappointed to be saying no, is Halley's head shake. "Sorry. I'm Faye."

I take a step back. "Sorry. I'm so sorry."

I retreat back to my corner of the bar. Occasionally, I glance over at her talking with the man. She sometimes laughs, but she never looks my way.

In the dark, at home, I count stars on the ceiling. In my childhood bedroom, I'd put up thousands of them. Every night, I'd find patterns in the way I'd arranged them. Count out in concentric circles until my eyes closed. Even years later, with a blank ceiling,

I could still picture where they had all been. When I was young, I'd spent hours making up constellations with Halley during sleepovers. We'd use myths we knew or sometimes our own stories that we'd spool out like threads of our imagination. In Halley's stories, girls were always lost, turned into lights, into flickers in the dark. I can still trace them all with my fingers.

We were sixteen when Halley disappeared. She was walking home from a football game. We were playing the Wildcats, our town's rival. Everyone was at the game. If I hadn't gone with my parents, if my little brother hadn't been playing, if we hadn't been waiting to take him out for ice cream after the game, if I'd asked her to join us and she'd said yes, if, if, if, I'd have been walking home with Halley. Her parents don't call to check if she's with me. No one reports her missing until well into the next day when I go over to her house to ask if she wants to come over for dinner. Her parents say she sometimes doesn't come home at night. That it's normal. They shrug at my insistence that she should be home. But my parents call the police when I tell them. They say it's better to be safe.

No one finds Halley Blackwell. It's like she stepped away from the stadium bleachers and right into another universe. There is no evidence. Just an Amber Alert with a picture of her that I took, because her parents don't have any of her, and her school photo makes her look older than she is. A police officer tells me that a photo where she looks girlish would be best. People want to save girls, he says. I don't say, *Don't people want to save everyone?* I wish I had.

And years pass. And years pass. In college, I imagine that she went to another school and that's why I never see her. I call her phone number sometimes, but no one ever picks up. And years pass. And years pass.

When I no longer think about Halley every day, when I no longer long to reach her, I still sometimes have nightmares that she is trapped underground. That some devil pulled her under the dirt. She calls out for me to help her, but in the dreams I'm always locked into my seat on the bleachers, I can't hear her over everyone cheering. If I can find her in the dream, it will undo the past. If I wake up, she'll be fine. If I call her, she'll pick up. If, if, if.

It's a week before I see Faye again. I hadn't thought about the interaction much. Usually, just before sleep, I'd see her face and try to find what I thought had been Halley's features. But memory rearranges us, and I couldn't be certain I was sure.

I'm grabbing a coffee before work and she's in the café I always go to. I don't notice her, but as I'm about to leave, she says, "You're the woman who I thought I was someone else."

I turn to her and it's still Halley's face. Her blue hair is pulled back into a bun, dressed professionally in tailored pants and a long-sleeved silk blouse draped so lightly on her it looks like the wind would turn it to shreds. I blush, feeling foolish. "Yeah, sorry about that. You really look like a friend I used to have."

"Scientists say that everyone is likely to have at least one doppelganger," she says.

I laugh, a little baffled. "Do scientists say that?"

She nods. "Something to do with a limited number of genes to compose humans. There are only so many facial characteristics to go around."

"Huh. Well, you're certainly my friend's doppelganger then." I move to leave.

"Would you like to get something to eat sometime?" she asks. "I'd love to know more about my lookalike."

I'm about to say no, to leave, not wanting to carry my mistake forward. But she smiles fully and I can see that her lower canine is cracked off. When we were twelve and playing baseball, a ball hit Halley square in the face. She'd smiled over at me, said, "I'm okay!" but blood had pooled down her face as soon as she spoke. She'd broken her lower left canine clean in half. So, to Faye, I say, "That would be great!"

I write my number down for her and she says she'll message me to set something up. When I get to my office, my hands are shaking. We'd met in first grade, the two girls in the back row of the classroom. She had a stuffed monkey with her. Benjamin was his name. I like monkeys too, I said, and she smiled. Back then, she was the shy one and I spoke too much. In our teens, we switched. I was all gangly limbs and awkwardness, and she was petite and precise and perfect.

At the office, my first client of the day is new. She runs a business consultation company. I wonder what a business consultation business does exactly, but I don't ask because I'm supposed to know those things, to understand how businesses operate. I tell her how our services work. Why her business should use one of our training sessions.

The woman frowns more and more as I speak. Finally she asks, "How do you guarantee that what you do works?"

"The answer is we don't, ma'am. We can't. I could point out studies we've done and how we've seen employee charitable donations go up after a training session. I could show you surveys we've done several months after the training where employees have listed off positive things they've done since. I remember one man who started volunteering at a children's foundation, and he talked about how much of a change he was bringing to those kids' lives. I can't tell you that our services made people more empathetic. No one can tell you that. Results for us are seeing positive changes, but . . . maybe that's not what you would consider working." I shrug. I've given this speech a thousand times, seen a thousand business owners have a moment's mental struggle over how they could react. No one wants to say charity isn't change.

She purses her lips, looks down at the floor, and then back up at me. "Positive results are certainly a huge thing. We would love to have your company come in and do a training if that is the impact."

I smile my biggest smile. The one I used to practice in front of the mirror. Genuine without being too much, too happy. "You really are working to bring light to this world, ma'am. We're so excited to partner with your company."

She smiles at that. We go over the paperwork quickly. Once they'd heard the speech, most people didn't have many questions. As she's leaving, she turns back to me and says, "What got you into this line of work?"

I don't know how to answer. My bosses had seen me give a presentation during college on how advancing robotics could be done not by advancing the technology but by advancing the amount of empathy people had for the robots themselves. The more like us an AI looked or sounded, the more we cared about it, the more we were willing to give it our information, let it into our lives. People would come up to me after and ask if I was looking for work after school. We train empathy, they'd said, and I'd laughed. I figured a friend was pranking me. But I'd looked up the company that night, and when I had graduated and was looking for work, I'd messaged them. I figured I'd be there for a year while I found something I actually cared about. And the years passed, until I couldn't imagine sending out resumés, writing cover letters.

"I suppose I wanted to help," I say to the woman. She nods, as if that is enough.

I call my brother at my lunch break. He's at work but he picks up. "Slow day?"

"I literally watched paint dry earlier. They're redoing one of the office wings," he replies. "What about you? You sound like you, but not."

I wonder what's in a voice that he could tell. "I think I ran into Halley."

There's a pause. Silence. Maybe he doesn't remember her, doesn't know who I'm talking about. "Missing Halley?"

"Yeah. Halley who went missing."

"You think you saw her?"

"This woman looks exactly like her, sounds like her, down to her broken tooth."

"Okay, did you ask her?" I don't need to see my brother to know that he has begun running a finger down the side of his desk, a thing he always did when he was thinking through something. After Halley went missing, he'd come to sit in my bedroom, cross-legged on the floor, and it always made me see him again like when he was a little, little kid. He'd never say much, just sit by me, as I stared out the window, trying to will Halley back home.

"She said her name was Faye."

"Okay, so maybe she didn't want to be remembered? I always kind of wondered if she'd run away."

He'd mentioned that once before, had pointed out how we always saw bruises on her, how her parents looked through her when we saw them together anywhere. And I'd wanted it to be true. That she'd simply left, become someone else in a happier place. But I'd thought she'd have said something to me, she'd have reached out, she'd have let me know everything was going to be all right.

"I . . . had that thought. But she really looked like she didn't know me. And she asked to get dinner, said she wanted to know more about her lookalike."

A long pause. "I don't like that. You shouldn't meet up with her."

I took in a breath about to explain why I needed to, why it was important, but he cut me off. "But I know you will. Just be on guard, Abs. Sometimes the people we remember should just be remembered."

Later, when my phone goes off, I think about not looking. As if not giving into temptation is an option. As if I haven't been scrolling through photos of Halley, looking for other clues I'll be able to spot in Faye. "Late dinner? — Faye."

I type back *sure*. A few moments later my phone lights up again. "I'm new to town. Suggest a place?"

I give the name of a restaurant that's a ten-minute drive. Far enough to be away from my home, but not so far as to be unfamiliar. I want to be on my own turf. She wants to meet in a couple of hours.

It's only as I'm changing, slipping out of business clothes into jeans and a t-shirt, that I realize the restaurant I picked is a Greek one. Halley's favorite food had always been gyros. We'd get them at a local diner and she'd eat them as if she was starving, picking at the meat with her fingertips, grinning. I was never a voracious eater, picking at salads, sipping water, but her joy for food was infectious. She'd say, you have to enjoy things, you have to let them fill you up. When she went missing, I think about all the things she enjoys. All the things she won't have. And then I push that away. She's not dead. She has to be alive. She still can enjoy things. If she ran away, if she hopped on a bus out of town, if she's living somewhere with a house and kids and a life that made her happy. If she never let me know, if she doesn't trust me to tell me, if I'd never know, at least she was okay. If, if. if.

She's already waiting for me when I arrive, sitting in a back booth, and staring out the window. It's dark out, but the sidewalks are well lit and I wonder what she's looking for. I sit down across from her and she jumps a little, pushed out of whatever thought she'd been in the middle of.

"Hey," she says. "I was just thinking about how people walking past windows must never think about what they look like to the people inside. Like not knowing what stories we might be daydreaming them into."

Halley had always known when I was wondering what she was thinking. She'd tell me before I even had the chance to ask.

"I think about people inside like that when I'm walking past. How I'm catching glimpses of them without knowing what they're thinking, what they're talking about." We both turn to look at a couple walking past. They are holding hands but not talking to one another.

"What do you like here?" Faye asks. She picks up the menu and begins glancing at it.

"Oh, I've tried a lot of stuff. It's all good."

She laughs. "Sounds like you're talking about life."

The waiter approaches before I can respond. I see her waiting to see what I'd order.

"A Greek salad and water please."

The waiter turns to her. "You, miss?"

She glances at the menu one more time. "I'll do the same. But a Coke instead of water. Thanks."

I want to say that she should try the gyro, but the moment is gone. She studies me and so I study her back. She's wearing different clothes—but equally expensive-looking—a long-sleeved and cowl-necked dress also made of silk. A simple gold watch. She looks as if she's come from a business dinner.

"What was your friend's name again? The one I look like?"

"Halley. Halley Blackwell." I say, but there's no hint of change in her expression when she hears it. It's someone else's memory.

"It's a nice name. Wish it were mine." She chuckles. "You knew each other when you were teens?"

"Yeah."

"But not since?"

"No."

She smiles, just a little, just at the corners of her mouth. More wistful than happy. "It's a shame that we lose the people we were friends with when we were young."

I nod.

"She must have been a good friend," she continues. "You looked so startled, but happy, ecstatic really, when you touched my shoulder. I wanted to be your friend then. Wished I was her. So I could continue that happiness."

"She was a very good friend," I say. "The best I ever had."

Our salads and drinks arrive, cutting the conversation. I want to thank the waiter profusely. The conversation felt like a trap, like standing at the edge of a chasm as someone tries to get you to walk closer to falling.

We both begin to eat. I pick at my salad, lifting up a single leaf to nibble at. Across the table, she does the same. It's like she is mirroring what I'm doing. I set my fork down and she does too.

"I noticed you broke your tooth. How did that happen?" I want to catch her off-guard, no time to make something up.

"Car accident," she replies. "Those air bags are menaces. Did you know they can hit hard enough to take an eye out?"

"I didn't know that. Wow."

She nods and her face looks older for a moment. Layers of makeup. Maybe she's much older than me. Older than Halley. Maybe this is all a mistake.

"What do you do?" I ask. Ready to just make conversation and be done with this.

She looks up from her food. "I'm a trauma specialist."

"Like a surgeon?"

She laughs, and with it she changes completely. It's a full-bodied laugh that shakes her shoulders. And I am seeing Halley laughing, almost falling off my bed because she'd remembered something stupid a boy had done in class. In the memory, I reach out to catch her. Do I catch her?

"Not a surgeon, no. Have you heard of Trauma Redemption Services?" she asks, the laugh leaving her body.

And I have. Of course. It's all the rage for the wealthy. I'd talked to people who'd had it done. They often came to empathy trainings, ran businesses, would ask me if I thought the procedure would make them less empathetic or more.

The theory behind Trauma Redemption was that if you had a traumatic memory erased, you'd lose something fundamental. So they gave it to someone else. It was taken from their mind and implanted into someone who would sit in front of them, letting the memory run through them, as the person watched. The person who had the memory now had to keep it. In case the giver ever wanted to recall it, wanted to talk through what had happened again, wanted to relive it on someone else's face.

"I have. What do you do with them?" I want her to be someone in the office, someone who typed up reports or moved finances around.

She looks out the window again, and her reflection on the glass looks younger. "The first one I ever did was someone who had crashed his car. Crashed the car right into someone else. He said to me, 'I never saw her.' But in the memory, he did. I wondered if he wanted me to know. If he  wanted to forget, but wanted to know that someone else knew?"

I don't say anything. And when she turns back to me, she still has Halley's face. It's older and sadder and lost in a moment of thought. But it's Halley. She smiles at me. "I have a procedure to-morrow. It's why I'm here actually. For some clients, we'll travel. I'd like you to see the procedure."

"Me?"

"Yes. I looked you up after we met in that café. Saw what you do for a living. It sounds like it might be an interesting thing for you to see, help your work."

I don't say, *But I never gave you my last name.* I don't say, *How did you find me?* I just stare at her and remember when we were twelve and it was my birthday party. Halley was eating cake and she started crying. I ushered her into my room and asked what was the matter. She was sad because she had been eating my birthday cake and had looked up and realized that I was getting older and she said *What if we keep getting older and we move away and we eventu-ally start talking less and less and what if we aren't friends in the future.* And I said, *But we're friends forever, Halley.* And she'd said, *Promise?*

"Okay, sure," I say.

Faye smiles. And then she changes the subject, begins talking about a movie she saw recently. We make small talk for another thirty minutes or so. Then she writes down an address and time and slips me the piece of paper. Her handwriting is perfectly straight and neat, like someone trying to write in a way that wouldn't be recognized.

"Oh, it's not creepy by the way. I saw the building you walked into after you left with your coffee. The company name. Only one Abby works there. The miracles of modern search capabilities." She picks up her purse carefully. "You can find anyone."

She leaves before I respond.

I count stars. Think about the constellation Halley had named after Persephone. She'd said, that one looks like it wants to run but she can't. I said, isn't that a myth about balance? Like we can't always have spring and we can't always have winter. Halley shook her head, it's a story about trying to forgive. She didn't explain. But every sleepover after, she'd trace the constellation with her fingers. On nights she isn't there, I do it for her.

Halley in my bedroom, stretching over the bed, about to ask me a question.

"Please don't forget tomorrow." A text arrives and I don't answer. But I think she must know I'll be there.

My brother sends me a message, asking how it went. I want to tell him everything, but I don't want him to worry. I don't think it's her, I type out. But I never hit Send.

ONCE, WHEN WE WERE IN our twenties, we watched a movie in which a young girl is kidnapped. It's violent, She screams and fights, but she's still snatched up and forced into a van. I didn't realize I was crying until my brother had placed a hand on one of my shoulders. So gentle I almost didn't feel it. I'd turned to him and he'd had tears in his eyes too. I never asked him if he was thinking about Halley or if it was only because he was worried about me. She used to call him Bro, every time she came over. She was at our house so often, it felt true.

*It might be her*, I type out. I hit Send.

I call out from work. The first time I've used a sick day in years. In the morning, I pace the kitchen, sipping the same cup of tea for hours.

There are no messages from her. I wonder if she wants to see if I'll really come, if she worries that pressure will make me stay away. I watch a video about monster movies, how creature effects evolved over time. It's background noise, but I find myself listening when a makeup artist talks about how hybrids scare us. "If something is close to something we know already, but not quite it, it makes us nervous. It's like the uncanny valley, you can be far away from being a human in looks and we'll be fine with it–a happy little robot, all beeps and boops, and square frame. But make it almost human, have fingernails, and teeth, and smile at us when we smile, but only then, never on its own, and suddenly we're terrified."

In university I designed a program that seemed like a simple game from the outside. You created an avatar based on a photograph of yourself, then you entered a little game sphere. You answered trivia questions, and a little robot on the screen would smile or frown depending on whether you got the answer right or wrong. But as you got deeper into the game, the robot began to look more and more like the game player. At first the changes were simple–the cartoony robot would get the player's eye color. But the game became more elaborate the more you played, and the robot's face shifted to the shape of the player's face. At the end, the player was playing a cartoon version of himself. My professor gave me an A, but he said he didn't understand the concept. I hadn't really known myself. Only that when I played the game, I never used my own photo. I used photos of people I loved. In the end, my mom or dad or my brother would be smiling at me when I got answers right. I never used photos of Halley.

The building could be anything. Just a rented-out office in the middle of the city. The café next to it is bustling, another office suite is filled with an accountant's office. I walk past to the elevator and go up to the seventh floor. A receptionist is dressed in a simple black dress. She smiles at me and asks my name.

"Oh, you're Faye's guest, right?"

I nod.

"Awesome! We don't usually have viewers, but she said your company is thinking of working with us? That would be so cool. Trauma and empathy go hand in hand."

"Not really," I say. But the receptionist is already not looking at me, instead playing a game on her phone. Tiny birds fluttered across her screen, diving to get coins that were falling alongside them.

I take a seat and wait. If I had gone to work today, I'd be just about on my lunch break. If I'd never said yes, I'd send my brother a photo of a coffee that I got from the place where the barista always swirled the foam into flowers, into the night sky, into anything he could think of. If I'd never gone to the diner, I'd be somewhere else. If I'd never been at that bar and I'd never seen her, I'd point out Persephone every night until one night when I forgot. If, if, if. Halley would finish walking home and she'd be home and we'd talk the next day about the football game and she'd lean over and tousle my brother's hair and say good job, Bro. And he'd let her. Only her.

"You can go back now," the receptionist says. And I follow her to a room that looks like an office, except it's been divided in two by a glass partition. A woman sits across from Faye. They both are on simple office chairs, and there's nothing between them. They are close enough their knees almost touch. A man in a lab coat stands to Faye's right. He holds something that looks like a cross between a needle and laser pointer.

The receptionist sits next to me. "Let me know if you need anything. These sessions can be hard to watch the first time."

"Only the first time?"

She shrugs, "You can get used to anything."

"What's the trauma?" I'm not sure I want to know, but I have to.

"The woman was kidnapped when she was a child. She has nightmares about it still. I don't know why she waited so long to have it removed."

The man in the lab coat moved next to Faye, pushed her hair away from one side of her head and I see a small metal plate right behind her ear. He uses one side of the device to pop the plate open, but I can't see if it's skull behind it or what. And then he places the device against her head and presses a button.

I watch her face. At first it's pain and then it's fear, and she cries and she cries. The woman watches her blankly. But the more Faye cries and pleads, the woman shifts in her seat, until she finally reaches out and takes hold of Faye's hands. She holds them gently as the rest of the memory floods through her. And then it's over. Faye's head droops, she stays sitting, and the man in the lab coat talks to the woman for a few minutes. They shake hands and another woman enters the room and escorts the client out. I can't believe there's not more. That she doesn't stay to ask Faye questions. If the memory is gone, does the woman feel free?

"It's over?" I ask the receptionist.

She nods, smiling. "So simple, right?"

I ask where the restroom is and once inside I brace myself against the sink. My hands shaking so hard I can barely grip. I look up and Faye is behind me. Her face watching mine in the reflection. And her face is Halley's face. Older. I try to look for laugh lines but I can't find them.

"How can you do that?"

She steps closer to me, until she's standing at the adjacent sink. She turns on the water. She rolls up her sleeves a little, and I see scars on her forearms, so many scars. "They're not my memories. I'm just holding them." She splashes her face with cold water. Grabs a paper towel and begins drying herself.

"Halley?" I almost whisper it.

She shakes her head. "I'm not her."

"I lost her."

"I'm sorry," she says. "Maybe our services could help you, too?"

She reaches out and touches my hand. Just for a second. As she takes her hand away, I see a tiny tattoo etched in the hollow of her wrist. A pomegranate. She sees me looking. "After Persephone. Do you know that myth."

I nod. "It's about forgiveness."

She smiles at me oddly, as if I've said something obtuse. "That's a strange interpretation," she says. And then she leaves. If she turned back, if she reached out again, if she whispered that promise, if she walked back to her office and back through her life until she was at the football game and she waited for me, she'd come with us, we'd eat ice cream, let it melt in our mouths, so sweet and cold. If, if, if she was Halley. If.

She doesn't come back into the bathroom. It's just me and the sink and the mirror. If I study my reflection in the mirror long enough, maybe I won't know who I'll recognize looking back at me.

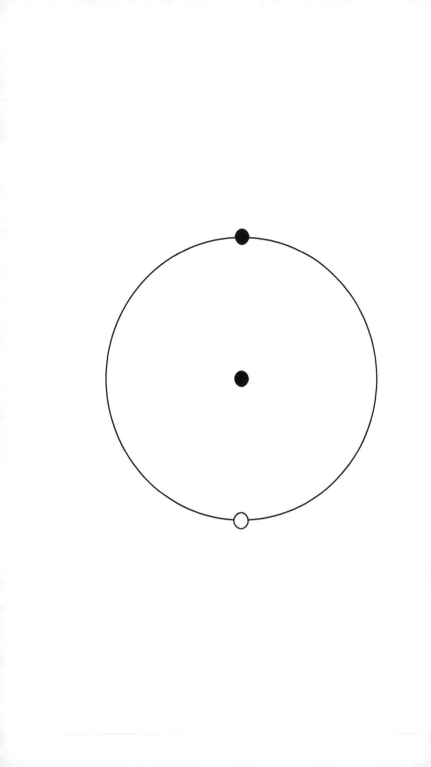

# Underwater Even Bells Sound Like Bodies

VIV DISCOVERED SHE COULD separate her arm from her body one morning while making pancakes. She remembered to leave clumps in the batter, ladled the batter onto hot griddle with practiced care. Her left arm, doing nothing useful in the operation, began to inch away from her. Starting at her shoulder blade, it popped itself loose with a sound like an air-filled paper bag being smacked between two hands. Viv stared at her arm as it crawled across the countertop.

She didn't swear or scream, because she wasn't the type. As a little child, she fell into a rattlesnake nest and lay so still, so fascinated by the mess of scaled and gently hissing bodies around her, that nothing bad happened. Her mother wondered if it was a miracle. Her father called it luck. Her grandmother said, "But, well, hasn't this one got a little witch in her."

Viv's arm stopped crawling when it reached the cookie jar. It was caught in a rousing attempt to open the jar by itself. "What the hell will you do with a cookie?" Viv asked, startled to realize that she was talking to her arm as if it was not a part of her. She corrected, "What the hell will I do with a cookie?"

The arm gave up, slinking back to her, knuckles drooping down in defeat. With one athletic leap, it reattached to her body. Viv finished making the pancakes and began to wonder how long her arm had been able to do such a thing. Did it leave her while she was sleeping? Go for moonlit walks? Paint pictures of the ocean, a place she had never seen in person but dreamed of so often that sometimes she woke up with her hair soaking wet?

She ate the pancakes at her desk. Her job was writing copy for travel sites. She wrote about areas she'd never seen. She imagined the trees south of her, hung thick with moss. She daydreamed beaches onto the screen. When people read her copy, they could feel the heat, the wind, the waves. They smelled food with spices that had never before lingered on their tongues. They heard voices, voices, voices. As she typed, she felt another pop. It was her leg this time, lifting itself away from the crease where thigh met pelvis. It stepped away from her, wobbly as a toddler on its own. She rooted for it to find its balance. Cheering when it bent at the knee to give itself a little less weight at the top. Her single leg hopped over to the window, leaned against the wall.

It didn't reattach until she was almost done with work and needed to pee. She asked politely and it rejoined her. She ate dinner alone that night, just her and her body. Her wife was on another long shift, texting her that she missed her, texting her that every patient she saw was worse than the last. She was a paramedic, but she just as well could have been an ice cream truck driver. She brought Viv solace but nothing else.

Viv took a bath, smoothed her hands over her skin. As a child, she'd never liked Barbies but had enjoyed disassembling them. She'd pop off an arm, a head, slice open a leg to see the frame that let their joints move. She was convinced that her skeleton looked the same. One day, she'd felt bad about the damage to the dolls, and she patched up the Barbies with bandages and tape and glue. She'd made a raft of twigs and sent them down the stream in the forest behind her house. She wanted them to be free of her.

When her wife gets home, Viv is already in bed, falling into dreams. Her wife molds her body to hers, warm and soft as the first day they met. They'd danced at their wedding, though Viv had no rhythm. But her wife had said, take some of mine, and suddenly Viv's feet had moved like a symphony.

"My body wants to leave me," Viv mumbled from her sleep.

"But you're the best place to be," her wife said.

In the morning, Viv went to the garden. She let her arms and legs step away from her. She lay on the ground, waiting. Her arm returned first, muddy from the banks of the river. Then a leg, sticky with sweat from learning how to run by itself. Then the next arm. The next leg. Viv sat up, watched the sky.

She texted her wife, "Let's go to the sea. Can we go to the sea?"

Her wife responded. "Yes, of course, yes."

Viv wondered how far out she could swim. If her legs and her arms might carry her all the way to the horizon.

# Static

WHEN WE WERE YOUNG, MY brother and I played in the forest behind our parents' house. Our father had given us antique walkie-talkies, inherited from his own grandfather. We loved to pretend we were an elite team sneaking through a wood filled with monsters. Dusk was the only time we played this game—never at night when it would be too frightening and never during the day when we wouldn't feel afraid. It was a game about edges: almost too afraid to play, almost too dark to see, almost able to convince ourselves that the monsters were real, or weren't.

The crackle of the walkie-talkies and our voices pitching through the half light of the trees returned to me often when I was older, in dreams usually. We'd had a code for monsters then: "The stars are out." A message to let each other know that we'd gone past our edge and it was time to find each other and go inside.

I would ask, as I crept through brambly berry bushes, pine needles pressing into my knees, "Are you there, Bravo? It's me, Alpha. Are you there?"

And then, always, my brother's voice, filled with static, would cut through the near night. "I'm here, Alpha, I'm here."

"THE SHALLOWER THE ROOTS of a tree," I said, "the more susceptible it is to drought. However, there are ways to combat this: breeding trees to have roots that grow deeper and faster or with thicker xylem. Drought is no longer an unexpected catastrophe. In point of fact, it's more expected than having a mix of rainfall and dry periods."

The woman I spoke to, Catherine Evers, was the head of a funding program, and she talked to dozens of scientists a day—all of them with eyes going full street urchin in the hopes that she'd give them just a little more leeway to pursue whatever noble goal they had in mind. I didn't like that tactic, though. It was better to just state the facts.

"And what exactly does your project do to benefit the trees, Ms. Monroe?" she asked.

Not "Dr." but "Ms." Noted.

"We're working toward creating a product that would act as a sort of steroid for xylem, essentially—making it stronger and more efficient."

"Shouldn't we be focusing on fixing the drought, not the trees?"

"Seeing the forest, ma'am, isn't always the best solution," I responded. I knew already that she wouldn't be funding us. "I work with trees, not weather systems."

"Ms. Monroe, I'm in the solutions business. Meaning that I provide solutions for research teams through funding, but also that I like to see that the place I'm funding is solution-oriented." I stopped listening and began to nod at points where I expected she wanted me to.

My brother had always been better at this sort of thing: handsome and charming, quick to laugh at jokes even when they weren't funny. I imagined that funders would leap at the chance to give him money. Working for the Institute, though, he probably never had to stretch those skills. Funding was as guaranteed there as a plant photosynthesizing.

Back at the lab, Karin saw my expression and sighed. "Another one bites the dust?"

Shrugging, I said, "Yep. Why can't you do these meetings?"

"You explain things better?" she replied.

This was probably true. Karin was the kind of scientist who had trouble un-sciencing her language. "Maybe Alec could go next time?"

"He'd just end up yelling at everyone and you know it. You're our only hope, Chetna."

"Well, then we're doomed," I said as I walked into the tree room. We had two rows of dirt beds filled with tiny saplings. I believed in the trees. I longed to see them survive. As the world got harder for them, I could feel it inside me, aching. It was hard to think of how tall a tree could grow when all you were looking at was its beginnings.

"How tall do you think it is, sis?" Akhil asked. He pointed to the tallest tree in the forest.

We were eleven, the age of showing off, and so I said, "Dunno, but I can find out."

"How?"

"Climbing it," I said.

"You'd never," he said. He expected me to use math, logic, or something to do with measuring distance and shadows. I was never the daring type.

I ran home and got the measuring tape. The climb itself was easy, as I had always been athletic. Halfway up or so, I looked out over the trees. Everything looked full of life, squirrels scurrying and wind rustling the leaves and birds chirping out warnings to one another—a stranger in their midst. Akhil looked so far away and small and young, younger than me. I couldn't see his worry, so I imagined that he was in awe.

I waved to him and that's when I fell.

I don't remember falling, just the rush of the air in my ears, then Akhil kneeling beside me. My father picking me up to carry me to the car, to the hospital. And Akhil holding my hand. He said, "It was my fault, Dad." I never knew why he said that. His hand was warm. It reminded me that I was alive and everything was all right.

THE MORNING AFTER THE funding meeting, I got the call. I spent most mornings running, getting up before the sun and taking off on a long jog. Long stretches of daily exercise were something my body had become so accustomed to that it was now more necessity than choice. Basketball had gotten me a scholarship in college. I enjoyed the movement of the game: the leaps and twists, the way everything could change suddenly. Basketball was rarely over until it was over. Life, in a way, was like that: the sudden twisting of the expected outcome into something else.

After college, though, I'd needed to find some kind of exercise to do on my own. To keep my mind clear. It's what I had found in exertion: a moment of clarity when I was at my physical breaking point. Running made sense. I ran for an hour every day, sometimes two—especially on weekends. Sometimes I missed the camaraderie of a team sport, but I didn't like being held to someone else's time frame. In running, one only had to count on one's own body.

I had three set running paths. My favorite went through the woods behind my apartment complex. In the mornings, there were rarely other people on it. I only chose it when I felt I needed it. Like a special treat, the doctor's lollipop after the shot.

The sun was beginning to rise and light shot through the trees, casting shadows around me. In my pocket, there was a buzz. For a second, I wondered if it was a phantom.

Few of the calls one gets at dawn are good. Slowing my pace, I plucked the phone out of my pocket. Without checking who was calling, I pressed Answer. "Hello?"

"Chetna Monroe?" An unfamiliar male voice, slightly mispronouncing my name, putting too much emphasis on the "e."

"This is. Yeah."

"This is Ross Spenceler. Of the Trow Institute." He took a long pause, letting that sink in. "There's been an issue with the research station. It's about Akhil."

"What happened?" I stopped running, felt my body adjust to the loss of forward momentum—a feeling in the pit of my stomach like the drop of the elevator, the dip of the car over a hill, the Ferris wheel swinging down.

AKHIL HAD BEEN THE FIRST at everything. The first to walk. The first to say a word: "Amma." The first to learn how to ride a bike. I was the watcher, first taking things in and only after consideration actually doing them. Where Akhil fell often, my steps were firm ones. Our mother said we should have been named "Steady" and "Ready." We didn't look alike. Akhil took after our mother: rounder face, more delicate features. I looked like our father: sharp and angular. An aunt had once muttered that it was a pity our genders weren't reversed. "It's okay to be a pretty man. Akhil will be all right. But a strong-looking woman? Tsk. Poor Chetna."

Akhil had responded to this overheard sentiment by placing a spider in the aunt's teacup. The shrieking had been delightful. Sometimes, one or the other of us would remember the incident and let out one of her shrieks: high-pitched and wailing. We'd both fall down laughing. It became a patented way for us to end fights. A promise, through laughter, that we'd always look out for one another.

The accident had been sudden. A bridge giving out. Hundreds of people died. Our parents had been driving home after visiting me. I always think of that part first.

"Get groceries more often, Chetna. Your eggs are three

months out of date!" My mother's voice, scandalized. That is what I remembered of the visit most, later when I was notified. I went to the grocery store after the call, filling the cart with things I'd never eat.

I put the groceries away, hands shaking, and tried to imagine my way back. Maybe time travel could exist, if I just tried hard enough. Then I could change it.

Akhil missed the funeral. He couldn't leave, he said. The Institute was going through something. Akhil hated funerals: as a child, he would hide in the confessional booth during them. I'd yelled at him, called him a coward. At the burial, I filled both of my hands with dirt to place on the caskets, trying to trick our parents into thinking Akhil was there as well.

We hadn't spoken since. It had been almost two years.

Sometimes, when I wanted to call Akhil, I'd instead look up the accident. In the years since, people had begun to speculate that it might not have been an accident at all. That it might have been the Shadows—an act of war unlike anything else we'd seen from them. There was no proof, save for uncorroborated reports of people seeing Shadows at the site afterward, lingering at the banks of the river and staring into the water. I had looked for them in photos of the aftermath, tried to see if I could spot one among the human faces. But in photos at night, it was too hard. Anyone could be anything.

AT HOME, I PACKED QUICKLY, THOUGH I wasn't quite sure what to prepare for. My flight would leave in a couple of hours. The Institute had booked me on the first one available.

I hopped in the shower, washing off the sweat from the run. The hot water hitting my face made me feel more and more awake. The awakeness brought questions: Why had the Institute told me so little? The phone call had been clipped, mostly just information on what plane to take and how soon I should leave. I should have known their protocol well, but maybe it shook me more because I'd never been on the receiving side of news from them.

My father always said that the Institute's personnel prized their ability to say things without revealing anything of value. Double-speak to the $n$th degree, he called it. I remember watching a program about Shadows with him, and a researcher from the Institute was being interviewed. She talked in negatives.

"We don't know where Shadows came from, only that they came from somewhere. We aren't sure where they first appeared or when."

It was only when her segment was done that my father turned to me and said, "What did she tell you about Shadows?"

And I realized I only knew what they weren't. You can paint a beautiful picture using negative space, but you can't use it to understand something. Not really.

My arms had turned red. How long had I been standing in the shower? I turned off the water, standing for a moment in the quickly dissipating steam, and watched water dripping down the sides of the wall. What had my brother gotten himself into?

I took a taxi to the airport. When I landed, a driver would take me to the research base. A long drive, I assumed, as the base was located fairly deep in the forest. I'd seen pictures, but I'd never been there. All those trees. All that darkness hidden behind the trees.

"SHADOWS?" I ASKED MY mother once. I was maybe ten or eleven. Old enough to have heard stories about Shadows, old enough to be scared of them. Our parents both worked at the Institute. Met there, actually. Our father had thought our mother was a secretary at first. Our mother was not a woman who enjoyed assumptions.

"It's something we've known about for years. They're not shadows like you're thinking, Chetna." Amma held her hands in front of the bedside lamp, making a shadowy rabbit on the far wall. "Not like this kind."

"Then what kind?" I asked.

She sighed. "It's hard to explain. They're shadows that are existing where they shouldn't. Shadows that don't belong in our world." She shrugged, reaching out to tuck a piece of my hair back. "We're trying to study them."

Always that word with the Shadows: *trying.*

LOOKING OUT THE PLANE window, I could see the forest in the distance below. As a child, I might have thought that the forest went on forever. Where was the base amid all of the darkness and green?

The airport was mostly empty. It was more a place that people left from rather than came to. A tall man, around my age or a little younger, held up a placard with "Chetna" scrawled on it. If I hadn't been expecting to see my name, I might not have been able to read the sign.

I nodded at him. "I'm Chetna Monroe."

He held out a hand for me to shake. "Liam Green. Are you set? We've got a long bit of a drive ahead of us."

I shook his hand, nodding. "Yeah. How long?"

"About six and a half hours." He'd already turned and begun to walk away, so he didn't notice the look of shock on my face.

"Six and a half hours?"

"Yeah, it's a jog into the forest. It's a no-fly zone, so we can't just helicopter you closer. Have you not ever been?"

"No, I haven't." I paused, unsure how much of myself to tell. "I've worked for the Institute, but only in an occasional and freelance capacity."

Akhil had always been more interested in the Institute. We'd both, perhaps inevitably, gone into scientific fields: his was astrophysics, and mine was botany. Akhil thought about the stars, about the future. I did as well. There was no future without plants.

He'd called me the day he found out.

"I got a job at Trow!" His voice made it sound like he was actually jumping up and down as he spoke.

"Oh, my goodness, that's brilliant, Akhil!" I was happy because he was so happy.

Liam and I walked briskly. I could easily match his pace. He led us into the airport parking lot and pointed out a Range Rover. "You're Akhil's sister, is it?"

"Yes."

He took my bag and tossed into the Rover's back seat. We got into the car. He was silent for a long moment, not starting the engine, just thinking. "I'm sorry," he said.

"He's just missing," I said.

I'D SEEN A SHADOW ONCE. DAD showed it to me, though he was probably not allowed to, when I visited the office he worked at. The Institute had offices around the world, small sets of researchers working on specific problems. Amma said it was like a web, the research radiating out from Trow. A Shadow had been caught in some sort of trap that looked like a mirror. A "shadow box" was what they were informally called, I found out later.

At first, I couldn't tell that there was anything there at all, just my reflection in the mirror.

"No, Chetna. Look at your reflection. Look closely."

I peered into the mirror, at my own face staring back, and then noticed that my reflection's eyes had silver pupils. I gasped and my reflection smiled.

"Dad, how can it look like me?" I was outraged. It was like it had stolen something from me.

"It's what they do when you catch one. People in my department say they just copy to blend in, like chameleons. But I think they do it because they like to disconcert us."

I looked away from the Shadow. I didn't like it. The way I knew it was watching me. "Dad, what do they want? Why are they here?"

"We really just don't know." He peered at the Shadow, thinking about something. The look on his face was an unfamiliar one to me: somewhere between sadness and, possibly, fear.

Years later, I'd wish, over and over again, that I had asked him more. Not just about the Shadows. About everything: his childhood, his memories, the dreams he had at night. I wanted to have enough stories of my parents that I could understand them completely, could tell myself some piece of them every night so that I might never forget them. I think they were happy people. They loved us. That was a lot to have known, but still I wanted more. Don't we always?

We didn't talk. The road into the forest was barely a road at all: unpaved and only wide enough for one vehicle at a time. Finally, I broke the silence to ask a question that was gnawing at me. "What do you do if there are cars going in both directions?"

Liam smirked. "Hope the other one runs off the road."

"Really?"

Liam laughed. "No, of course not. The road is almost only used by people from the base. We know where everyone's going, usually. We can avoid collision. I suppose if there ever was a situation, the person with the more off-road vehicle would go off the path."

"What's the base like?" I looked out at the forest. The trees were so dense that it seemed dark, almost as dark as night, though I knew—the way one can know something in a logical way even if one's mind is screaming about how wrong it is—that the sun should be up for a few more hours.

He took a moment before answering. "I think it's an interesting place. I work mostly in documentation. I'm a photographer, so maybe I don't see as much as some of the science-minded. But it's quiet."

"Do you . . . do you work with the Shadows much?" I asked.

Liam took his eyes off the road for a second to look at me. "The shadows? I'm not sure what you mean."

"Aren't they mapping the Shadows? Isn't that what they do there?" I wondered if Liam was messing with me again.

"Uh, is that a code name for one of the projects or something? I was told the base mostly did ecosystem research." His voice sounded honest, if confused.

"Yeah, sorry. I'm so used to speaking in the terms of the Institute. Ecosystem work, yeah." What exactly was going on? I wished my parents could tell me. They had always known the best way to explain things. I studied Liam as he kept his eyes on the road. Did people who didn't grow up thinking about the Shadows become oblivious to them? Years and years ago, they were considered a huge threat to everyone, but now Liam didn't even make the connection. I opened my mouth to ask more, then stopped. Maybe he was keeping secrets, and maybe I should keep my own.

THE BASE SANK BACK INTO its surroundings, giving it less of a camouflaged look and more of a defeated one. It was as if it had struggled to stand out but failed. I wondered if the design was on purpose.

"Base, sweet base," Liam said.

"It's less . . . impressive than I expected?" I said, hoping that by making my words sound questioning they wouldn't cause any sort of offense.

Liam shrugged. "I kind of like that. We're kind of, I don't know, *of* the forest? Instead of *in* the forest?"

I nodded, glancing around at the trees that surrounded us,

dense enough for anything to be hiding within their embrace. These trees were different from the ones I'd come to love on my daily runs. Not only their height but also their stillness. These were trees that never bowed with the wind. I made a note to explore them later, after I knew where Akhil was.

Liam continued, maybe sensing that I didn't completely agree with him, or at least didn't understand quite what he meant. "You know architecture at all?"

"A little. The famous stuff, sure."

"The base reminds me of that Frank Lloyd Wright house, Fallingwater. It always looked like it was supposed to be there, just another rock jutting out." He shrugged. "Maybe I just got used to the base and I'm making shit up in my head."

I smiled at that. It was the kind of self-doubt of my own analysis that I sometimes felt but would never dare speak. "No, I get it. That makes sense."

I followed Liam into the base. I'd asked to speak to Spenceler before doing anything else. Few people were in the open, so I had no idea how many were currently stationed there. We went through hallway after hallway, all of them seeming to loop back onto each other until I couldn't remember which way would lead me out. Was that intentional design?

Finally, we stopped at a door.

Liam pressed the intercom. "I have Dr. Monroe, sir," he said.

The door made a clicking sound as it unlocked. Inside, a man in a suit sat behind a large desk. He looked in his forties, with silver hair and black-rimmed glasses. It looked like he had chosen his look from the *Distinguished Doctors* catalog.

He stood up, extending a hand for me to shake. "Ms. Monroe, pleasure to meet you. We spoke on the phone. I'm Ross Spenceler."

Taking his hand, I nodded once. I'd looked him up after the phone call and discovered that he was in charge of this particular Institute base. This was information he hadn't offered on the phone, that he was Akhil's boss, and it made me distrust him. I'd assumed I was being called by a liaison of some sort. The blankness of his office, not even any photos on his desk or generic art on the wall, added to this feeling.

"Can you tell me what happened with Akhil?" I asked, badgering my way through preliminaries.

"Of course. Take a seat." He gestured toward one of the leather chairs in front of his desk. I sat down. Liam stayed standing behind me. "Liam, you may leave. I'll buzz you when you can come back to escort Ms. Monroe."

"Buzz me?" Liam said, with more than a hint of displeasure. But Spenceler had already written him out of the room and didn't seem to notice. Liam nodded once at me as he left and said, "See you later, Dr. Monroe."

As the door clicked closed, Spenceler lifted a remote control off his desk and pointed at the wall. A vid screen appeared. On the screen was Akhil's face, staring into the camera.

"This was found in your brother's belongings. It was labeled as a message for you." He pressed play and the vid came to life.

"I'm into something here with the Shadows," Akhil said. The vid skipped for a split second. An error, or had something been erased? "The trees. When you look at the way the leaves are. There's a story there." Again, the vid skipped. I wondered if Spenceler had edited it. I assumed he had. I glanced at him but his face betrayed nothing. "And when I think about it, I know that I need to go out there. I need to find them and talk to them. But, Alpha, the stars are out."

The vid shut off. I stared at the black screen. Akhil had looked unwell. His normally perfect hair—something he'd half-jokingly and mostly very seriously prided himself on since he was a teen—was disheveled, and his eyes had dark circles surrounding them.

"Do you understand any of what he said?" Spenceler asked.

"Not much. I know a little about Shadows, of course. My parents were some of the—"

"Pioneers in the field. We were quite excited to work with Akhil because of that. Do you understand anything of the rest of the message or why it was left for you?" Spenceler's gaze didn't leave mine. He was waiting for me to give something away.

"Well, I'm his sister. His whole family, basically, now. So maybe that's why? I don't understand much else, though obviously we're in a forest and I'm a botanist, so that might explain the stuff about trees." I crossed my legs and kept eye contact with Spenceler. If he was looking for a flinch, he wouldn't get it from me. "Now, I'd like to know what happened to him. Where you think he is."

Spenceler sighed. "We don't really have any idea. He was doing some fieldwork in the forest. Basic day-to-day, and he always returned at night. Then he didn't. We tried to use his locator, but it was either turned off or broken."

"Did you send out a team to look for him?"

"We did." Spenceler broke eye contact.

"And?"

"They didn't come back."

At that, I flinched. "What?"

"That was almost two weeks ago. All of their locators disappeared from our radar."

I took it in. Akhil had been gone for almost half a month, in a forest so large that anyone lost in it could conceivably never be found. In a forest where Shadows lived. Akhil, at five, turning to me with a grin and a frog in his hands. Akhil in the forest.

"Why did you bring me here?"

"Because we think you can find him," Spenceler said.

WHEN I WAS YOUNG, I USED to believe that blood connected you. If I were honest, though, I'd admit that my belief had gone beyond a feeling of familial connection and into the realm of the supernatural. I used to believe that Akhil and I could sense each other. As if, across miles, we'd know what the other was feeling. Sometimes I thought that if I could just clear the static from the air around me, I could even hear his thoughts.

When Spenceler told me what the Institute had created, it made me think I hadn't been so wrong at all.

"We're calling the prototype a Sangtraceur. We'll change the name if we put it on market, but the scientists seem to like the duality."

"Blood tracker?" I asked. He had explained the device in vague terms, just enough so I'd know what I was getting into. Essentially, it was something I'd physically ingest, and afterward, if I got close to someone whose blood had similar genetic markers to mine, then I'd know it. He avoided explaining how I'd know, even when I asked, which made me nervous. It was always the "other possible side effects" that were the worst ones in science.

"I don't really understand how this could be marketed," I said. "Wouldn't it only work in situations where the missing party had a blood relative available to assist?"

"Technically, no. We're working to develop it so that we could use a blood sample from the missing person. Unfortunately, we have no such samples of Akhil's blood. At this point, it's somewhat of a long shot even using you. We only thought to try because you're twins."

I was willing to try anything.

ONLY ONCE WHEN HE WAS at the Institute had Akhil and I ever really talked about Shadows. He had come to visit me. I'd shown him around the lab, introduced him to all of my trees. Their scientific names and then the names I gave them that no one else knew about.

"Do you think the Shadows do that?" he asked me.

"Do what?" I was absentmindedly running a hand along the trunk of Portia, a small juniper.

"Personify things. Name them."

I'd never wondered about the Shadows' inner lives. Never even imagined them having any. So I just stared at Akhil. Waiting for him to go on.

"They must have dreams too, right?" he'd said, but it wasn't a question so much as a wish.

I ATE IN THE BASE'S MESS hall that night. Liam sat next to me, perhaps taking his chaperone duty a little too seriously.

The base's food was exactly what I should have expected from a well-funded facility: the kind of cuisine found in fusion restaurants with three-star reviews, designed by people who didn't understand the cuisines they were fusing. I hated it.

The way Liam stared at his plate made me think he had similar misgivings about chilaquiles made with a mint-and-seaweed mole. I was about to ask him when a blond woman walked up to me.

"You're Akhil's sister?" she asked.

I nodded. "Chetna."

"I'm Rebecca Halprin. I was on Akhil's research team." She held out a hand for me to shake. I didn't like her use of the past tense, but I shook her hand anyway. "I always wanted to meet you!" She said it brightly, but it raised flags for me. I could sense there was more gossip than interest behind her comment.

"What were you researching exactly?" I asked.

She stared at Liam for a beat too long, though he didn't notice. "Ecosystems."

"What about ecosystems?" I asked. She narrowed her eyes at me, as if to say *Not in front of the help.*

"I'm sure Akhil told you about it" was her measured response. She emphasized the *sure.*

I wondered if she knew how little Akhil and I had spoken, although she must have. She left, and I was glad to see her gone.

"They don't like saying much around me," Liam said. I hadn't realized he'd been paying attention.

"Why not?" I asked.

"Probably because I'm not a part of the Institute exactly."

"But you work for them?"

"No, not at all. I told you I did documentation and photography. I'm technically being paid by the government to document Trow's progress. They're required to have an outside, unbiased person to do the documentation. Something for their funding, I guess." He shrugged. Maybe he was someone who didn't like asking questions of life. It was possible he was the kind of person who knew that in some situations, the less interested you seemed, the more you'd be able to find out. But he didn't come across as having a duplicitous side. "You know, there isn't a lot for me to do, so they end up assigning me to random tasks. Pick this person up, look through these files for errors. It's their dime, I guess."

Was there really so little to document? I wondered if the government was worried about what the Institute was doing. I'd have been worried.

"Dad! Dad!" I'd yelled when I couldn't find the Shadow in its box.

He came running, Akhil close behind him.

"It's not in the box anymore," I said. The panic made my voice come out alien—sharp and high-pitched, more girlish than I'd ever sounded, even as a child.

"We've had to move it, Chet, it's fine. It just had to be moved back to the Institute," Dad said, soothingly.

I'd dreamed it escaped, had hovered over my bed and stretched its fingers out to touch my face. In the dream, I'd been unable to move, to fight, as it caressed my cheek, a smile cutting across its face to emphasize the emptiness of its eyes. That's why I'd come to check on it. The shock of it not being there made my heart thud against my chest. My pulse raced so hard that my throat hurt.

"What if it gets out and no one's watching it there?" I asked.

My father placed a hand on my shoulder. "The Institute knows how to handle Shadows, Chetna."

Later that night, Akhil and I played crazy eights, which I rarely lost and so always wanted to play.

"I'm going to join the Institute," Akhil said.

I looked at him. There was a conviction in his voice so solid that the words seemed corporeal as they came from his mouth. "Why?"

He studied his cards. "To keep us safe. From the Shadows. I'll make sure they don't get out, Chet."

He was making a promise, and I was afraid that he'd keep it.

I COULDN'T SLEEP. THE BASE'S silence was so unfamiliar to me. I crept to the window of the room I was in, not wanting to make a sound, to break the noiseless night.

There were no stars out, reminding me that Akhil's video had warned me of monsters. The darkness was absolute. I waited for my eyes to adjust, to get some sense of what was out there. The shapes of trees beckoned, somehow darker than the rest of the darkness, like the shade of black paint that absorbs all light. These were not my saplings, not the trees I knew and cared about.

For the first time, I wondered if Akhil could be alive out there. It was a question I hadn't allowed myself. Whenever I had missed him over the past two years, I had comforted myself with the thought that he was alive, that I could sense him across miles.

But I couldn't sense him then. It was like one walkie-talkie was too far away and all I heard was the buzz, the buzz. The buzz was better than silence, though.

IN THE MORNING, WE SET out. Spenceler was providing a small team to go with me. He didn't say it was for protection, but I figured that was the purpose. I was surprised at the lack of fanfare, of planning. It seemed unlike the Institute to rush anything. Again, I wondered what they weren't telling me about Akhil and about just what he was researching. Why the rush? The willingness to call someone in who didn't belong to them?

The application of the Sangtraceur was simple, almost as painless as testing blood sugar levels. One prick. I'd imagined it would feel momentous, but instead I hardly noticed it.

The team comprised Liam and two others—a compactly built woman, Grace, and an unusually tall man, Samuel. Together they looked like a dance team in an absurd comedy. Grace was on the same team as Akhil, she explained, and knew the area we were heading into. Samuel was security, but I noted he lacked weaponry of any sort. I wondered if Trow's security used something other than guns.

I wasn't sure why they'd included Liam. It seemed unlike the Institute to have an outsider, and he had seemed slightly bemused when I asked why he was joining. This bending of protocol made me feel more off-balance than I expected.

Grace had an easy laugh, and I wondered why she was working for a covert scientific base instead of somewhere in the sun—a garden or some other place where her laughter wouldn't have echoed so strangely. She talked about various trinkets of subjects as we walked.

We had to walk—the trees were too dense to drive through—and dead leaves crunched beneath our feet. Something about the trees bothered me.

"I've always been a fan of boba tea, but your brother hated it. I suppose you know that, though," Grace said. How we had gotten onto tea, I wasn't sure, but my mind sprang back into the conversation at the mention of Akhil.

"He did? I don't know that we ever really talked about tea much."

"He said he had an aversion to things that felt like frog eggs—as if he knew how frog eggs felt." She let out yet another peal of laughter.

"He did, though," I said, smiling.

Akhil and I must have been only four or five and walking in the woods behind the house. There was a stream that ran through it—a gentle one that we could cross without worry of getting tossed about or pulled under, so our parents trusted us to walk near it by ourselves. Once, we'd spotted a clutch of frog eggs between some stones and we'd both been fascinated. Before I could say anything, Akhil had reached out and grabbed up an egg from the edge of the mass. Then he walked back toward me to show me.

But he was small and didn't know how to hold things, and the egg was smaller and didn't know how to be held. Somewhere in the steps back to me, it slipped between his fingers, fell back into the water, and was pushed along the stream. When Akhil realized, he let out a soft "No."

We looked in the water, tried to find it, to return it to its siblings, but the egg was gone. Akhil had stared at the water with such a look of loss. At the time, his sadness felt larger than I could carry.

WE HAD BEEN WALKING FOR hours, and I had felt nothing. Maybe the Sangtraceur was a faulty experiment. Maybe my blood wasn't strong enough. Maybe some connection was lost. I wanted to pause, to lean against a tree and just think for a moment. But the tree trunks looked less inviting than my trees back home.

Grace and Samuel had gotten ahead, were talking quietly. Once in a while, Grace would nod and glance back at Liam and me. Were they talking about things they didn't want us to overhear?

"The trees are bothering me," Liam said.

"Me too. Something's off, and I can't place my finger on it."

"Same. It's like I'm seeing every bit of the puzzle but not the picture it's supposed to make."

It seemed to be getting darker. I wasn't sure if it was because it was later in the day than I realized or if the trees were becoming even denser. While dense forests often had more foliage, as trees needed to drink up the light in any way they could, the branches and leaves here went further down the trunks than seemed quite right.

Liam paused. He bent to the ground and picked something up with a frown.

"What is it?" Grace asked. She and Samuel must have paused and noticed us dawdling.

He held out the object that he'd picked up. A red cherry, stem and leaf still attached. "This seems . . . out of place."

I looked up and understood why the trees had been bothering me.

Earlier it hadn't been as obvious. The variations had been only slight: birch with bark a little less smooth than it should have been. But here the deception was failing completely. The leaves were wrong. The trees were wrong. A few of the tree trunks looked like species of pine but had leaves—oak leaves and plum leaves. Fruit hung alongside pine needles on other trees that had the trunks of oaks. The trees were all wrong. "What the fuck . . . ?"

"What?" Samuel asked.

"The trees—" I began.

Liam cut me off. "They're mixes. Impossible mixes."

As he said it, I felt something strange. It was like something was moving inside my veins—a pulse that wasn't my own pulse, traveling through my body, slowly getting stronger. If I had to name it, I would say that my blood felt like it was screaming.

Grace frowned and walked up to the nearest tree, a pine. She reached out to touch the trunk. As she did, a burning sensation hit me in the head. It felt like a migraine bursting into life, but more intense and instantaneous than any I'd ever had before. *Other possible side effects*, I thought for a split second before the pain seemed to rip open my skull.

On my knees, without realizing I'd fallen, I clutched my head.

Liam rushed to my side. "What is it?"

I couldn't see through the pain. Only flashes of light. Then I heard someone scream, and I wasn't sure if it was me.

As the world soared into darkness, I thought I saw the trees bending toward our group, as if reaching down to grab us.

IN MY DREAMS, MY MOTHER often braids my hair. I haven't kept it long in years, but still, in dreams, she can braid it. She tells me stories about Shadows. She says, "Don't be afraid, Chetna."

In the mirror, my Shadow smiles at me.

In my father's office, he kept drawings people had done of Shadows. He told me, "Maybe they've always been here. Every culture tells stories of people who aren't people—the fair folk, the angels, the women who slip out of the river at night. Maybe that's always been them."

I was so afraid.

Akhil tells me, "If we can map them, then we can understand them."

There are so many things we've never been able to map completely: the bottom of the ocean, the brain while it dreams, other planets.

My mother smooths hair back from my forehead. She says, "You're safe."

OPENING MY EYES, I WASN'T sure how long I'd been out. Above me, the trees seemed to stretch up forever. I rolled over onto my side and came face to face with Grace. Her eyes stared blankly back into mine. I held in a scream, jumping to my feet. Grace's body looked fine, as if she were just watching clouds. Her face though was like an absence. Her eyes wide and not seeing. Her mouth was opened slightly, as if she were about to speak but had no words. Samuel and Liam were gone.

"Liam!" I yelled, hoping for but not expecting a response.

Silence. And then, "Chetna!"

I spun toward the sound. Liam was sitting against one of the trees, a couple dozen yards away. I ran to him. His face was pale and his breathing shallow, but he was alive. "What the hell happened?"

He shook his head. "You went down, and then Grace was screaming. It looked like . . ."

"Like?"

"Like a tree branch had grabbed her. It squeezed her until she just stopped moving. I don't know where Samuel went. I think something hit me." He winced, the talking aggravating whatever injury he had.

"Okay, we're going to get out of here." I helped him to his feet. He leaned heavily against me, glad for my height and build. "Can you get us back to the base?"

He nodded, groaning as he did so. We moved as quickly as we could, the forest growing darker around us. I listened for any sounds that might be Samuel. There was nothing.

"Why were the trees wrong?" Liam asked. "How was that possible? Trees don't just—"

"I don't know. Don't talk, save your energy." I didn't say what I was thinking, remembering that Shadows had learned to mimic the looks of people. Why couldn't they have learned to mimic the looks of trees? Why couldn't they be spying on a base that was supposed to be spying on them?

○

It FELT LIKE WE HAD walked for years, but I finally began to recognize that we were getting closer to the base. The trees were returning to normalcy, regular leaves on branches they should have belonged to.

Liam saw it first. "Oh fuck, fuck, fuck."

The base was gone. Or not gone, but overgrown. Tree branches burst through the windows, grew out through the roof. Hundreds of trees. There were still vehicles outside though. But only a single Jeep hadn't been overturned by roots. The overturned vehicles reminded me of dead insects, how their bodies always seemed to turn upwards, legs curling in.

We made our way toward it, and as we got closer, I could feel the tingling in my veins again. That *pulse, pulse, pulse* that was both not my own and yet as familiar as a voice I'd known since the day I was born. I dared not give in to it. If I dropped from the pain, then Liam would be stranded as well as me.

Pulse. Pulse. Heart beating so hard that I could feel it through my own palm when he held my hand after the fall. Two pulses, racing at the same tempo.

Then I saw the body. I thought it was someone from the base. Except there was something so familiar about the curve of the body, the hair. "Akhil!"

I wanted to run, but Liam couldn't, so we limped closer. Akhil looked peaceful, eyes closed, but his clothing was ragged and filthy. There was a scream in my throat that I couldn't release.

Then his chest rose, once. He was breathing. Shallow, hiccupping breaths, but he was breathing.

I got Liam to the Jeep, and then I went to Akhil. His eyes moved beneath the lids. He was dreaming. I dragged him toward the Jeep, managing to get him inside. Liam said he could drive, though he looked like he was fooling himself. I let him, wanting to sit by my brother, make sure he stayed breathing. Listening to his breath, it sounded like the safety of home.

THE INSTITUTE TOLD ME that no one was left alive on the base. They didn't go into details, for which I'm thankful. What the Institute said was that Spenceler had gone off the grid. He was supposed to be mapping Shadows, but he'd decided to try and capture them instead, use them for something though no one said what. He saw the forest as some kind of perimeter he could control. They said they sanctioned nothing. I didn't believe them. I think they knew that I didn't. An anonymous donation of funds was sent to my research team the day after the call. Enough to help us through a few years of dedicated study, at least.

Liam and I kept in touch. He asked me once, when he was still in the hospital, if I thought the Institute had him accompany me because they were hoping to get rid of him. I'd wondered the same thing, or if they were hoping he'd convince the government to increase their funding. The dead can tell us nothing though, so I shrugged and said, "Maybe they just wanted me to feel comfortable." And we both laughed at that.

He left the government and began to work as a photojournalist. His work surprised me, capturing light and dark in new ways. He would've been good at photographing Shadows, but I don't think he'd like to hear that.

Akhil slept. He continues to sleep. Doctors tell me that he might never wake up. Comas are strange. Sometimes a person wakes up after ten years, or ten days, and sometimes they never wake up, just eventually go from one kind of sleep to another.

I may never know what he discovered. I may never hear him tell me the stories of what happened to him. Any stories. He had figured out the leaves, but why did he go back out into the forest? Still, I think the Shadows returned him to me. They hadn't killed him. That said something, but I wasn't sure what.

Occasionally I catch a glimpse of my reflection in a darkened train window, a bathroom mirror somewhere the lights aren't shining bright enough, and my reflection will smile back at my frowning face. I never know if they're watching me to see if they made the right choice, or if they watch everyone and I'm the only one who notices. When I can, when there's time before the tunnel opens, before the light pulls my reflection away, I'll stare back. I wonder if it scares them when I smile.

Often, I visit Akhil in the hospital. I sit by his bed and tell him about my life, about the research into Shadows being done, the advances made. Mostly, I end up watching him breathe. I don't know if I'm cutting through the static at all, but still I tell him, "I'm here, Bravo, I'm here."

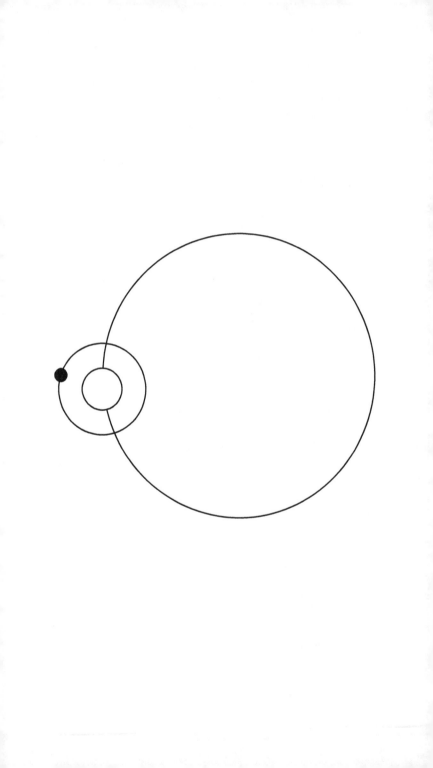

# Red as the Night Sky Burning

ON MARS, WE DON'T BURY the dead. The bodies are burned in a contained facility. No ashes are let go with the wind. We're told to add nothing to the soil. No signs of our intrusion. As if burying a body would be so much different from building structures, digging into the ground to plant posts of steel. Each body, once burned, is sealed into a metal can, meticulously labeled with the statistics of the person's existence. The thought is that we will return them to Earth one day, to their families, to places where they can be let go.

Our days are spent mostly on work. All of us have our set duties. Mine is the garden, as I was the designated botanist on our mission. I tend to the plants under thick layers of glass ceiling and walls. Monitoring nutrients, ph levels, the level of dryness. Even in the greenhouse, with monitored watering, the soil dries out faster than it should. It's as if it can feel the winds and dusts of the planet. We mostly grow survival crops, heavy with nutrients or ability to fill one up: potatoes, squash, some leafy greens for vitamins and quick turnaround times. I also planted tomatoes. I dreamed of sun-ripened tomatoes back home, still warm from the sun when you bit into them. That burst of tangy brightness on the tongue.

The greenhouse is only one building away from the building where bodies are handled. The official name is the crematorium, but none of us call it that. We each have ways of talking around what it is. I went in there once, walked among the cylinders of lives once lived, and studied the names of people from missions before us. I knew their names, had read up on them all. I could attach memories of their faces in photos to the neatly typed names. Carrie Anders, age 34, was a redhead with a gap tooth, and two children back home. In every picture of her, she looked mischievous, like she would have been a delightful handful as a child. Tarsem Hollins, age 42, was a man with wide-set eyes and a smile that only could have been achieved through years of braces and care. He was married, and in every photo of him and his wife, they were smiling at each other instead of the camera. There were so many names. Every mission lost a few people—through accident, through illness, through the way that the planet could eat and eat at you.

○

WHEN THE GHOSTS BEGAN TO show up, none of us believed that we were seeing what we were seeing. A child running down a hall, her laughter trailing echoes to us. A woman leaning against a wall, smiling at something to her right. I saw my first ghost while I was tending the plants. My hands dug into wet soil as a little boy wandered in. He looked at me and I looked at him. There were no children on the mission, of course. Never had been nor would be. Still, I spoke to him as I would have any child who wandered into my greenhouse back on Earth, "Can I help you?" He shook his head, smiled, and ran past me and through the wall. I sat down, expecting to faint, but didn't ever feel anything come swooping over me.

More ghosts began to show up over the next days. Everyone began to see them. Elderly folks playing chess in the living quarters. Children playing hide and seek. A man pacing up and down the halls, thinking about something troubling. The adults never interacted with us, but the children sometimes did. They had faraway looks when they did, as if they suspected we were imaginary, a daydream playing out before them. How boring we must have been to them, then.

"Why not our dead?" one of us asked, gesturing to the building that housed the deceased. If any ghosts should haunt us, shouldn't it be the ones kept locked up here. We had no answers at first, though later I had my suspicions.

A woman in the greenhouse, red-headed and gap toothed, leaned against a plant table. She trailed a finger along the edge of a tomato plant, absentmindedly. She looked so much like her mother, though now a little older than she ever got to be. A mission twenty years past. I stood next to her and watched her staring off at something. A memory, the ghost-flicker photography in the mind of someone she loved. I wished I could reach out to her, wished I could say, we have her safe. We'll return her to you one day. But the young woman was already gone. The greenhouse empty. Just me and my tomatoes, reaching toward the sun.

On Mars, we don't bury the dead. We're told to add nothing to the soil. But what of our breath and voices, and the way we fill the night with our dreams? How they must reach out past the dust and wind, trailing toward the sky, reaching toward Earth, as if to say, please, we were here, we are here, you can see us if you look.

# Supernova

I USED TO SEE HER AROUND, at the cafés on campus or sitting by the edge of the lake. We'd had a class together, but it was one of the large lectures and she always sat a few too many rows away from me. I'd heard her name and said it sometimes under my breath because I liked the way it felt in my mouth: Cherry Smith. It felt so accidental, like halfway to the name of a superhero.

SHE HAD A HABIT OF SUCKING the end of her pen in class or in the cafés as she leaned over a notebook. I practiced saying hello, in my head, Hi, I'm Ava. My name was short, but it still got stuck on my tongue.

WHEN WE FINALLY MET, IT was at the library where I worked. I was shelving books on astronomy. "Did you know the bigger a star, the shorter its lifespan?" someone asked from behind me. I turned and it was her.

"I just shelve them, I don't know them," I said.

She laughed, though I hadn't meant to be funny. So I smiled back as she asked, "Does anyone know the stars?"

WE STARTED GOING TO MOVIES together. They were cheap on campus, and though the seats were usually sticky with spilled soda, the screen wasn't bad, and in the dark, everything else fell away anyway. Afterward, we'd walk around, talking over what we didn't like. I wasn't sure how we'd decided on it, but we never talked about the aspects that we enjoyed, only the flaws, what stuck out to us, pushed us away.

WE SPENT A MONTH LIKE THAT, always ending the night at my door. I'd wave as she left, a flick of my hand up, biting my lip to keep from asking her in. I didn't have the words to ask what we were, what I might have been to her.

AND THEN ONE NIGHT SHE asked, "Don't you want me to come inside?" And I stepped aside so she could. She looked at the few pieces of furniture in my tiny apartment, ran her fingertips over the back of the couch, then took my hand. When she kissed me, all I could think of were the tips of the pens, how she tapped them against her lips before taking them into her mouth.

ON THE COUCH, SHE KEPT kissing me. Our tongues dipped between each other's lips. I slid my hand under her shirt, traced the small nub of her nipple with my finger. She pushed me back, and I thought I'd done something wrong. As always, I was quickest when it came to apologize for things I might have done. But she slid a finger over my lips, pushed me back fully, and slipped her hand under my skirt.

IT'S STRANGE TO SAY that I don't remember how we slipped away from one another. How one day we talked a little less and then less still. How the other girls I dated after her started to take larger shape in my memory. How when my wife once asked, "Who was the first person you loved?" it took me a bit to remember her name. Maybe we never really take account of those slow untanglings until the knot has already come undone.

I almost never think of her. Though sometimes I see a young woman by a lake and the light will hit her just so. Or I'll notice someone suck the end of their pen, and for a split second I'll remember her. That moment of her mouth moving against me. I had sworn the ceiling flew off the apartment, up into the sky and away, until I was staring up at the night.

# Jumpers

THE DISTRESS BEACON WENT up and I assumed it was a drill. There'd been three in the past six months. New protocols or some such. I was in the sick bay. Migraine again. Or the start of one—that crisp preciseness that took over my vision, like I was wearing binoculars. Doctor Prentiss just told me to lie still and count to twenty-five until the meds kicked in. Twenty-five seemed precise but I bet she counted slower than me, because I was on seventy-three and my vision only got lighter and clearer as an aura covered me.

The beacon rang shrill. The ship was set up so that a distress beacon signaled in every room varying by the emergency importance of the room. The sick bay's siren was like a baby screaming at the top of its lungs while being hooked up to an amp. This would mean starting over at one.

"Lex, you're on call-up," Prentiss said to me. She stared at her vidbox where a message was scrawling across.

"I have to get up?"

"It's not a drill, apparently. Or they're really upping the procedure. There's a pod out there. I have visual on it." She touched her screen, dragging her fingers apart to enlarge the Out-cam, and a pod filled the image. It looked damaged: cracks on the side and the name was covered in scorching or something similar.

"Shit." All I could think to say.

"Migraine or not, you better go. This is your time." Prentiss might have been complimenting me or she might have been mocking me. I'd never heard her voice change tones.

But it was my job. I had one skill that set me apart from just about everyone in the entire space program and certainly everyone on the ship. I ranked as the best pod-jumper alive. There had been tests, timed trials, different scenarios thrown at me and I only ever missed one pod. There were few things more dangerous than an unmanned or out-of-op pod floating near a ship or station. No one knew what they might do; there was always the chance that they'd pop. A design flaw if ever there was one, but it happened rarely enough that it never seemed to get fixed. What I did was jump through emptiness, through space, and catch pods. It was a little like blowing bubbles off the Eiffel Tower and then parachuting after them in hope you could catch one before it burst.

○

I MADE IT TO THE SIT room. Lieutenant Halpern paced. He was a gold-medal pacer. "Lex, excellent. You saw the pod?"

I nodded.

"We need you to jump it. We've signaled them. Three times. No ping back. So we're to presume the crew is a nonentity or, at best, incapacitated. We need you to clamp them, and be extra freaking careful, Lex. The cracks on the pod already look dangerous."

I nodded, again, already picturing the jump in my head. The pod was roughly 90 feet from our ship and at an almost 110-degree angle from where I'd be jumping out. I'd have the corded clamp in one hand, my only tether back to the ship. I could see it perfectly. There'd only been one jump that I hadn't been able to picture beforehand, and it was also the only jump I'd ever missed.

Halpern helped me into my suit. The clunkiness was deceiving, of course. The bulkiness was what kept a jumper on track—including tiny implanted weights that could be manipulated for redirection mid-jump. Too light and we'd spin.

Halpern retreated behind the air-lock, and the bay door opened. I had three seconds to arc my jump. I arced right and felt the safety of the ship fall behind me. My sister had once asked me what it felt like, was it like being underwater? It was like being underwater if I'd been swimming in the center of a squall in the middle of a snow globe. Space contained me just as it was trying to pull me apart.

I pirouetted my body, shifting myself enough so that the pod was directly in front of me. Every jumper did it differently. One, I knew, looked like she swam through space. Mine wasn't as graceful: a combination of kicks, punches, and some moves that proved why I'd gotten kicked out of the ballet academy.

Closer, the pod looked even worse. The cracks and dents were deep and grooved, and they pockmarked the surface. I adjusted the clamp in my grip, placing it too hard against the pod would almost definitely lead to a pop.

The name of the pod was mostly obscured, black smudges running across it, but it was Bn-something. The pod window was dark, either because the lights had been turned off for energy conservation or something had malfunctioned. The darkness of the window stunned me. It was darker than dark, as if someone had siphoned the light out of the pod. Peering closer, something moved behind the pod window.

I let go of the clamp, yelling inside my helmet. I never jumped with my audio on, hearing someone talk you through a jump was like being talked through breathing. If you thought about it, then you weren't doing it right.

The clamp began to drift and I grabbed it, quick, but it sent my jump slightly off and I spun too hard. Instinctively, I pushed a hand out to brace myself as if I were falling, then felt hardness as my hand tapped into the pod with too much force.

My life didn't flash in front of my eyes. No birthday parties, first kiss, graduation montage for me. Instead, I saw the jump I didn't complete. The woman in the pod screaming for help, hands pounding against the window as I floated past her. I was too far away to clamp her pod. Too close not to see the panic on her face as she realized what was about to happen. There had been a ten-minute window, and her oxygen was running out. I had had one jump. The ship would pull me back but without time to jump again. All I saw was her face, panic, panic, and then something else. She gave up so quickly.

The pod didn't explode. None of the cracks deepened. Inside my helmet, my breathing went fast and shallow. Everything I was trained not to do.

I placed the clamp, gently, keeping an eye on the pod window. But I saw nothing. It must have been a mistake, a visual misprint.

The clamp cord went taut in my hands, signal having been sent by its sensors, as the ship began to pull us in. I ran a finger along one of the grooves. It was deep and smooth. Not a crack, but some kind of scratch.

Pulled into the bay, I waited until the door was completely closed before letting go of the clamp. The ship floor felt wobbly underneath my feet. Jumps always made my legs go weak, trembly. I stepped back to take a look at the pod, which reminded me of an insect husk.

The air-lock door opened; Halpern, Meerkin, and Prentiss walked through. Pulling off my helmet, Meerkin muttered something.

"What?" I asked.

"You look blotchy," Meerkin repeated.

"Huh?" I checked my reflection in the helmet visor. I was blotchy. "Had a close call, must've made me breathe too quick."

"Jesus, Lex. That's why you should use audio. Your jump looked fine," Halpern muttered.

I shrugged, keeping an eye on the pod window. Half of me expected some alien claw to slam against the glass. Nothing.

Halpern walked up to the pod door. "Scan for contams first, Doc?"

Prentiss walked up with her scanner. She ran it over the outline of the pod door. The scanner beeped and booped. "It's clean." She stepped back.

Halpern popped the door. For a split-second, I thought about running.

Inside the pod was darkness. A four-person unit, for short-term trips. Mostly exploratory, landing teams, or the like. There was no good reason for it to have been so far into the Out. Halpern shone a light inside. Two people were harnessed in. A woman and a man. They seemed so still, as if someone had painted them into the body of the ship.

"Lord . . ." Meerkin trailed off, unable to finish whatever dismay might have been following.

Then I heard it. Like a valve releasing, a low whining hiss. One of the bodies was breathing. "Someone's alive."

Prentiss hopped into the pod, doctor-mode activated, and put her hands onto the necks of the crew. "Her pulse is faint, but it's a pulse."

There was a rush of movement. I helped Prentiss and Meerkin take the woman to the sick bay. Halpern stayed with the pod.

Under the sick-bay lights, brighter than anywhere else on the ship, the woman looked even worse than in the darkened pod. Her skin drained of color and her lips held a bluish tinge.

Prentiss hooked her up to several monitors, as Meerkin and I watched, helpless outside our expertise.

The woman pulled in a shuddering breath, her whole body shaking with it. Her mouth opened a little, almost as if she were about to say something, and a long, black, tendril pushed its way out from between her lips.

Meerkin jerked backward next to me, Prentiss shrieked jumping away from the woman. The tendril reached further out, tentatively wiggling as if looking for something to grab onto. Another pushed out of the woman's mouth and then something emerged, using the tendrils to pull itself out. It looked not unlike a plant of some sort, all tendrily leaves, except that it was the purest black and it moved on its own. It jumped, tendrils propelling it forward, and landed on another table. And then in a thud it was over, Prentiss slamming a scalpel down into whatever it was. The tendrils shriveled in on themselves, forming a loosely shaped ball.

"What in the name of fuck?" Meerkin muttered.

I watched the woman. Her breathing had normalized; whatever it was hadn't killed her. Prentiss prodded the thing on the table. It made a crinkly sound, like it was dry or brittle.

"I think it's a plant," Prentiss said.

"A plant?" I responded. I'd never seen a plant come out of someone's mouth.

She peered at it closely. "Just from a glance, that would be my guess. I mean, I'll have to run tests, but . . ."

"What about her?" Meerkin nodded toward the woman. "If it's a parasite, could she still be infected or contagious or whatever?"

Prentiss glared. "Because I know everything instantly about an organism that may never have been seen before?"

Meerkin glared back. He pointed at the woman. "They probably saw it."

My migraine was coming back, waves shuddering across my vision. "I'm going to go check on Halpern. Give him a heads-up about there possibly being something living in that pod." I wasn't sure if they heard me over their dueling gazes, so I left without another word.

HALPERN WAS STILL CATALOGUING the pod. He was talking into his vid for every object he'd taken out.

"Halpern, have you found anything weird?" I asked upon entering the bay.

He didn't look up. "Weird?"

"There was a . . . thing . . . in the woman," I said.

He frowned. "On the woman?"

I shook my head. "No, in the woman. Like it crawled out of her mouth."

That made him look up. "Shit, did you catch it? Is it quarantined?"

"Prentiss stabbed it with a scalpel. So, yes."

He put a hand to his head, rubbing his temple vigorously. "Okay then. By that definition of weird, I haven't. I'd say I found something odd though." He reached down into the pod, pulling up a standard armband vidscreen and tossed it to me. "Pull up the most recent mems."

I did. The woman filled the screen. She must have taken off the band so that she could point it at herself. Her skin was pale and darkly blotchy. Her eyes tired. She talked directly to the screen. "I just keep going back to it. To her. You know? How easy it would've been to say sorry, apologize for it, and I didn't. All those years we could've been together and I just couldn't say sorry." She pulled in a shuddery breath, the kind that comes before crying. "I'm saying it now, if anyone ever finds us. I'm sorry."

The vid went black. I looked up at Halpern, and he was holding another vidscreen. Must have been the dead man's. "I didn't think hers was anything. Just assumed she thought she was going to die and needed to tell someone her secrets. But his is . . . well." He tossed it to me.

The man was oddly handsome when alive: angular face and large eyes, like a good-looking praying mantis. He stared into his vidscreen with a deep intensity. "I'm going to be quiet. Mara's asleep. I don't want to wake her. She should rest. We have so long to go. But I needed to . . . oh god, how do I say this? I never meant to hurt him. He was my friend, we'd trained together. Jumpers have a code. I thought it would be funny, just making it a little loose. But god, I'm sorry. I'm so sorry."

The vid went black. I wondered what he'd loosened. Jumpers had a million ways they could get hurt, and when it wasn't training and was an actual operation, those million ways to get hurt became a million ways to get killed.

"So it's weird, right? Them both having these confessional videos?" Halpern asked.

I nodded, thinking about it. There was something there that I couldn't put my finger on. I helped Halpern continue logging inventory, but it didn't come back to me.

○

PRENTISS FILLED US IN on the status of the woman: she hadn't woken and her pulse was getting weaker.

The status of the thing was even more inconclusive. Prentis thought it was definitely a plantlike organism, but she didn't want to make any guesses. "Possibly parasitic fungi of some sort."

We'd all heard stories of a station that had been overrun by a mold of some sort, killing the entire crew, but most of that was hearsay as to whether it had been parasitic or the crew had just died from inhaling it.

In my bunk that night, I fell asleep thinking about the vids I'd watched. I dreamed of something, a jump maybe, but didn't remember it upon waking.

The next morning, I checked in with Halpern. He'd finished inventorying the night before. The pod was emptied. "Where's the body?"

"I released it." He pointed to the airlock doors.

"That isn't protocol," I said.

He shrugged, "Possible contamination. I'm not taking chances."

Halpern was a rule-stickler. He'd always been one. I noticed a dustiness along his hands, like he'd bruised them. "What did you do there?"

He looked down at his hands and I saw him swallow hard, eyes widening. "I . . . uh, I don't know." He pushed his hands into his pockets. "Do you need anything, Lex?"

I shook my head and left.

PRENTISS WAS EXAMINING THE thing under her microscope when I went into the sick bay. She didn't look up, just asked, "Migraine?"

"Just checking in." I walked over to the woman. Her breathing was almost non-existent. The monitors showed an erratic heart-beat. Weak. I studied the pattern across her face. Blotchy bruising along her cheeks, dusty in color, just liked I'd remembered from the vids. The same dusty color as Halpern's hands. "Prentiss?"

"Yeah?" She still hadn't looked up.

"Do you think that the man on the vid could've died from the same thing and the . . . plant . . . could've been in the pod?" I asked.

"You mean two of them?"

I nodded.

"Well, I don't know. Possible I suppose, but if Halpern didn't see one . . ."

"What if he didn't know? Like it wasn't as big or something?"

Prentiss sighed. "You and Meerkin are going to drive me insane with your questions. I can't know everything about alien species. I'm not a xenobiologist."

"Sorry, I was just looking for hypotheses."

Prentiss glared. "I don't hypothesize."

IN THE NIGHT, I HEARD someone weeping.

"THE TENDRILS CAN DETACH," Prentiss said. She'd walked into my room without me noticing, and I jumped.

"What?"

"They can detach. I think it's set up like a . . . Have you ever seen a spider plant? Where it grows the little baby plants free of soil and they just sort of hang down from the 'mother' plant?"

"Sure, in pictures."

"Well, it works similarly, the babies are the tendrils. So, I think there could have been a smaller one on the pod theoretically," she said. "Now, I need to know why you asked."

"The bruising pattern on the woman. Well, I saw a similar one on Halpern's hands. Fainter, but it was there."

Prentiss leaned against the wall of my bunk. "The woman's dead."

"When?"

"An hour ago. Just stopped. Everything in her shut down."

I looked at Prentiss, trying to gauge what she was thinking. "What do we do?"

She shook her head. "I try not to hypothesize."

HALPERN DIDN'T COME OUT of his bunk. I knocked and he told me to go. He sounded like he was crying.

PRENTISS USED HER CODE to override Halpern's security door. He was curled up on his bunk, clutching a pillow, eyes swollen and puffy.

"I didn't. Oh god. It wasn't supposed to be like that. I was trying to save her, but she was fighting. People always fight when they're drowning. She kept hitting my hands away and I just . . . I just . . ." He couldn't finish, breaking down into sobs.

The bruises were dark on his hands. Prentiss had me and Meerkin help her get him to the sick bay.

"I'll monitor him. One of you needs to put out a distress signal."

I SENT OUT THE CALL. THERE was a ship two days away. We could last two days.

HALPERN WAS IN A coma by morning. I was in the sick bay when it happened, grabbing meds for a migraine. I saw movement out of the corner of my eye, but too late to shout. Prentiss was leaning over him, checking his pupils' reactions to a light, when it came out of his mouth. This one was smaller, quicker, and it was on Prentiss' face before either of us could react. Up her nose and she screamed. She fell backward and, as she did, more came out of Halpern's mouth. They came in waves, jumping out in little batches. Screaming, I ran from the sick bay, hoping the door closed quick enough to keep them inside. I looked through the door window at Prentiss rolling on the ground, gasping. After a moment, it was over. She started breathing normally and struggled to her feet. I watched her walk over to the medicine cabinet. Maybe, I should have guessed what she was going to do, but still I yelled "no" as she injected herself with something.

It was quick for her, at least.

"WHAT ARE WE GOING TO do?" Meerkin asked. We had both suited up. Me in my jump-suit, he in his normal suit for pod flight. We hoped our masks might keep them from getting in.

"The ship's contaminated now. We can't bring a rescue here. We can't let this spread."

Meerkin nodded. "I have an idea, sort of."

THEY SEEMED TO BE everywhere—tiny black shapes jumping in and out of my view. I wondered what they'd make me see. What final babblings they'd coax out, though I had a guess. A woman pounding against glass. The realization that I'd miscalculated, always cocky, always thinking I could correct my brashness, and then floating past.

○

THE RESCUE SHIP WAS ROUGHLY four hundred feet away. It was Meerkin's idea. He was a good person. I'd never befriended him, and I was sorry for it.

"We both don't have to die," he'd said. "You stand the best chance. You can warn them what's aboard."

I'd never made a non-training jump that far. Honestly, I don't think anyone ever had. But I let Meerkin think that he was sacrificing himself for something that was an actual hope.

WE DIDN'T REALLY SAY GOODBYE. He just told me that he'd be watching. I looked out and saw the ship, a speck slowly moving toward us. I closed my eyes and tried to picture the jump. Nothing.

I chose a simple spin. The one I'd done most. Nothing flashy. For a second I felt like I was falling, the pleasant zooming of a jump, and then my mind reminded me of why I was jumping. I wondered what the plants were. What they wanted? But maybe that was wrong. To think they wanted something. Maybe that's just what they did.

As I spun forward and forward, the ship getting closer, I pictured the woman. Her hands on the glass. I'd wanted to say sorry to her. My jumping coach told us that sometimes we'd miss. That was just the way of jumping. A lot of times it wouldn't be our fault, it was just that we weren't supposed to make that jump, for whatever reason. Still, I'd have said sorry if I could have.

I hoped she'd have understood. In the darkness, as I jumped toward rescue, I thought that maybe she would have understood. Maybe, she'd even have forgiven me. That's all anyone can ask for.

# The Ocean Is Not Empty

THERE WAS A CRACK AT the bottom of the sea. The man I loved saw it, right before he was swallowed by it.

WE MET AT AN ART GALLERY. It was an exhibit of photographs taken by astronauts after they'd returned to Earth. I expected there to be something different in their perspectives, something tangible that would come through in the photographs. Mostly though, they were exactly what one would expect: landscapes, children, the occasional flower.

But there was one series of shots that made me stop. They were all of shadows, in the corners of rooms, cast under streetlamps, in the backseats of cars. There was something eerily compelling about the images.

"It's like looking into an absence," someone said from behind me. I turned to the man who'd spoken. He was handsome in a way that had never particularly appealed to me—like he belonged in a commercial for orange juice or yogurt.

"An absence?" I asked.

"Yeah, like the shadows are the emptied-out versions of someone's life. Like there should be someone, maybe a child, sitting in that back seat, right?" he said.

That was what I'd been thinking too. That there was some sense of loss in the photos. "I can see that, yeah."

The man, smiled a little embarrassed. "Sorry, I realize I just totally interrupted your viewing space. I just . . . those images."

I nodded. "You didn't interrupt."

"I'm Joe," he said, extending a hand.

"Andra," I said. I took his hand and shook it.

Three years later, on the day before our wedding, he gave me a box. I opened it and inside was one of the photographs from the show. It had been my favorite of the photos: a little girl sat cross-legged on the floor of her bedroom and a shadow seemed to hover right behind her, as if it was watching over her. I'd never told him that it was my favorite of the photos. It was the one that felt more comforting than the others, as if the shadow was some sort of guardian.

"Where did you find this?" I asked.

"So much internet searching," he said. "This was the one you stared at the most."

"How do you know that?"

He laughed, "Because I was staring at you."

I WAS STARING AT THE photo three years later when Joe got the call. I'd been working on a report about a study at the lab where I worked. I heard him talking in the other room. His voice held the slightly deeper tone he used when he was trying to hide his excitement. I walked into the doorway to look in at him.

The vidscreen was open, and the woman talking to him was one I didn't recognize. Joe was smiling widely, even as he spoke.

I went back to my office and waited to hear what the news was.

"Babe, I got it," he said a few minutes later. "I'm on the team."

He'd been interviewing, for months it seemed, for a position on a submarine research team. They were going to be studying a rift that had appeared in the floor of the ocean. A crack, he'd explained to me, as if someone had pushed two plates apart—except there were no fault lines there. I'd never seen him so excited about working on something, so I didn't think about him being gone, about the danger, I just let him grab me into a dance around the room.

ON OUR HONEYMOON, WE STAYED in a hotel by the ocean, and every day we took long walks along the shore. He'd tell me different facts about the ocean every time.

"The ocean is kind of like a museum. There are so many sunken artifacts, ships, detritus of human existence. There are more sunken objects in the ocean than there are objects in museums."

"So it's kind of like a big trash heap? Or your aunt's attic?" I asked.

"Think about all those things lost. So many of them must have meant something to someone at some point. All those lives sunk in ships," he replied.

We both looked out at the water the waves crashing and rising and crashing. I wondered what he saw when he looked at the water. If he saw only the possibilities of what it could hold, while I just saw the blue stretching out and out.

○

"We don't know anything about the ocean, not really. Like we understand maybe ten percent of what's under the water and that's if we're being generous to ourselves," he'd said on our first date.

"How is that possible?" I'd asked. I was still unsure why I'd said yes to a date with him. There was nothing about him that was my type, beyond his looks, he was also a marine biologist, a science field that I'd never been interested in, preferring always to look to the stars, rather than stay on our own planet.

He shrugged. "The ocean doesn't give up its secrets easily. Does space?"

"Sort of. We can map it and photograph it and our physical explorations are getting further and further out," I said. And then I paused. "No. It doesn't. We can see these things and we can study them, but until we get out there, get our feet on other planets, we're never really going to know them. Not in the way that I want to know them at least."

"That's how I feel about the very bottom of the ocean. I'd give so much to just step into that abyss. To feel it beneath me and around me." As he spoke, he closed his eyes for a second, as if he was trying to conjure up what he was talking about. He looked like someone dreaming.

When he asked for a second date, I said yes.

"Yes, I understand, but I want to speak to someone else," I repeated.

The woman on the vidscreen looked as frustrated as I felt. "Ma'am—"

"My husband is on that submarine. I want to know what news there is. I'm not a fucking media outlet. I am his wife." Contact with the submarine crew had been out for over a week. No one could explain to me what might be happening. I'd only found out when the rest of the world did—in a tiny news segment scrolling past when I'd been watching for something else.

"I wish I could tell you something, but I honestly don't know anything," the woman said.

"Does anyone?" I asked. "Please?"

The woman's face broke slightly. It was a moment of compassion battling its way through. "I'm sorry, we just don't know."

○

"I DON'T KNOW," I TOLD my lab mate, Karissa. "He's smart and sweet and I like the way he thinks. But I'm not sure I'm looking for something serious."

"So why does it have to be serious? You've only been on a few dates," she said.

"Because . . ." I sighed. "Because I feel like I want him, more than I've wanted anyone else."

Karissa laughed. "Don't be an idiot, Andra."

I felt my face heating up, so I turned back to my screen. I was working on a virtual progression of some images we'd received from a space exploration pod. The photographs were weak—bluzzed out where we needed them to be clear.

Karissa spoke again, her voice softer. "I just mean, you always talk about work like it's the be-all and end-all. Like you can't have a serious relationship and work. But you can. You shouldn't lose someone just because we're going to discover something awesome. We're amazing enough to do both."

I turned back to her. "Thanks, K. I'll keep that in mind." I tried to sound sarcastic, but I was thinking about the way that the bridge of Joe's nose wrinkled right before he laughed at something.

THE LAST TIME I SPOKE to my husband he was laughing. They were about to descend and then I wouldn't speak to him again for a month.

On the vidscreen, he looked so happy that I wanted to screen-capture every moment. I wanted to paste the photos of him, laughing like that, all over my walls.

"Listen to this, love." He opened the window and I heard the ocean behind him. "I'm going to be under all of that."

Later, I queued up ocean sounds to fall asleep to. I slept so well that I did it for every night that week.

"DID YOU FUCKING HEAR ABOUT last night?" Karissa greeted me.

"No, what?" I asked. I couldn't tell if she was delighted by something or horrified. Her eyes were so wide and voice so high.

"We've gotten approval for the mission to Goldilocks!" She shouted the words.

The Goldilocks planet had been all we'd been talking about for the past two years. All the data coming back had been positive. "Jesus."

I had to sit down, a swooping feeling in my stomach, and I felt suddenly dizzy with it.

Karissa whooped with joy. We'd be working on the first mission to a planet that could likely sustain human life. The mission would be unmanned, of course. Exploration by humans wouldn't come for years. But the images coming back would be the most important, possibly, to ever appear.

My stomach fluttered and I pressed a hand to my abdomen, as if that would calm it.

THE GEL ON MY STOMACH WAS cold and when the doctor pressed the machine over, I flinched with the iciness.

"Do you want to see?" the doctor asked.

I shook my head.

"Are you sure about this?" she asked me.

I nodded.

I NODDED, TRYING TO PROCESS the information. "But you don't know who the survivors are?"

The woman shook her head. "We only know that some managed to get into the emergency pod. There was a distress signal as they were coming up. It could be one person. It could be up to seven people."

I nodded, again. I felt like a bobble-head. No ability to do anything but agree to everything I heard as if I comprehended any of it.

"We'll let you know as soon as we know anything."

"WHAT CAN YOU TELL ME about the conditions of the images?" I asked.

It was seven years since my husband didn't surface from the lost submarine. The images from Goldilocks were back.

"They're not great, honestly. You have your work cut out for you," Karissa said. "When are you coming in?"

"Tomorrow, I think. I have one last thing to do here, then I'll catch a train back tonight," I replied.

I'd been in meeting after meeting. We needed more funding

and my face was the best for pleading, our higher ups had decided. I wondered sometimes if it was because I looked so pathetic. I knew that everyone could read the loss on my face.

But the last thing I had to do was not for our company. I was meeting another widow of the submarine team.

Her name was Alison and her son was named David. He was a teenager now, but he'd been only seven when his father had gone into the sea and never came back.

We met at a café. Alison looked better than I did. I wondered if it was because she had a child, she had someone she had to be completely there for. David was a handsome kid, tall, with a mop of hair that hung over half his face. She recognized me as I walked toward them, and they both stood up to greet me.

I'd met her years ago when our husbands left. She'd been a bright, smiling woman, tiny and energetic. We'd talked about our jobs and joked about having space from our husbands. She'd said, "I'll finally able to read in peace." I don't know why I remembered that so clearly.

"How are you doing?" she asked.

"I'm good. Yourself?"

"Good, good."

We exchanged pleasantries, catching up on lives that didn't matter to ourselves. Then I just asked what I'd wanted to all along, "You've heard about the tape?"

She glanced at David, for the smallest of seconds and I wondered if he knew. "Yes."

"They said it's only a couple of moments of audio."

She stared at her water glass instead of me. "Are you going to listen?"

"I want to, yes. I'm angry the government kept the tapes quiet so long," I said. This was a lie. Angry didn't begin to cover it. I'd screamed at the person on the vidscreen when he said the audio tracks would be released, when he'd admitted the organization had them the whole time, but had been analyzing it before providing it to the public.

"Yes," she said. "But I don't know if I can."

"I don't know if I can either. But I know I can't not."

She smiled, and it was the saddest smile I'd ever seen. Her eyes held such a weight within them.

We changed the subject. Talked to David about his plans to become an astronaut. I gave him the names of some contacts if he decided to pursue them. At the end. Alison hugged me.

"I hope you find what you're looking for," she said as they left. I didn't understand what she meant.

THE REPORTS HAD BEEN vague. The survivors suffering from some sort of mass amnesia—the doctors called it a rare side effect of extreme trauma. But I never bought it. I assumed the company had paid them to be quiet. The only thing I'd ever seen with a cause mentioned was something about a shadow in the water.

They gave the families the audio before releasing it. I sat in my bedroom, lights off, and turned it on.

There was bluzzes of a static interference. And then it was Joe's voice. Of all the people to be speaking on the tape, it was him.

"Jesus, what is that?" he asked.

"It looks like—like a pool of ink?" someone else said. A woman. Her voice soft, scared.

There was a sound like the creaking of beams in an old house.

Then Joe again, "It's an absence."

Then silence.

THEY NEVER RELEASED THE TAPES. Maybe a family member had requested it. But I think it was because the audio offered no answers, just questions, just something to be feared.

I thought of it, all those decades and decades later, when they released the thought-vids of the crew of the Charybdis. All those young astronauts' last panicked moments as they crashed into the Goldilocks planet. The first manned mission, and I'd lived to see it. And I'd lived to hear the horrors of them screaming as they lost their lives for our curiosity.

The world wept with their families. Losses like this felt like everyone's losses. I remembered the strangers who'd sent me messages after Joe. I never read their words.

AFTER THE FIRST TIME WE'D slept together, we lay in his bed and I talked about what I did. How I pulled images from darkness and blur.

"I try to make us see what we shouldn't be able to," I said.

"You're like a fortune teller," he said.

"What do you mean?" I asked.

"That's our future, isn't it? Space?"

And I'd liked that way of describing what I'd did. I'd say that to people later, that I read the tea leaves of space.

I DON'T KNOW WHY I went to the gallery. They were doing an exhibition on Exploration. It was five years after the Goldilocks disaster. I was in my nineties. I had to have the home nurse go with me.

There were vidscreens up, paintings, but also a series of photographs. Those, of course, were what I went to first. A series of photos of astronauts right after they returned to Earth. Pictures of smiling faces, triumphant faces, and then one that made me pause.

It was of a man, on the ground, staring up at the sky. His hands clutched the grass around his body, as if holding on would keep him from falling back into the sky.

"What do you think he was thinking?" My nurse asked.

I took a long time to answer. "I think maybe . . . he couldn't believe he'd found his way back."

She nodded, as if she knew what I meant.

# We Are Still

WE WATCHED A BARN BURN down on the same day my grandmother sent me a message telling me, *you make your own happiness.* We'd been driving for hours, closer to the border but not yet there, when we saw it. A single barn licked with flame in the middle of a field. So many barns we'd passed had been long abandoned. Fields gone fallow, left to seed.

WE'D TALKED ABOUT IT: how many farms around here had been sliced in half by highways, home on one side and livelihood on the other. Those highways we no longer needed quite as much. It reminded me of something a friend had once said, reading an article about war, *We are a world who keeps cutting ourselves into smaller pieces.*

THE BARN WAS OLD, SOME parts caved in, though we couldn't tell if that was from the fire or from time. We stopped the car, got out, walked closer and closer. We wanted to see the damage, or I did and assumed we both did.

ONCE, AS A CHILD, I'D PLAYED hide-and-seek with myself. I wanted to know how long I could stay away, enclosed, before I gave up and ran out into the light. I tucked myself into the corner of my mother's closet, the heaviest of her dresses hanging against me. At some point, I fell asleep, only waking when my mother grabbed me into her arms. *We looked everywhere for you, we thought you were lost.* And as I hugged her, suddenly scared, suddenly filled with the thought of what it would be like to be lost, away, I said, *I'm still here.*

THE FLAME CREPT THROUGH THE barn, seemed to know where it wanted to be, keeping itself contained to rafters, then to walls, as if to slow the inevitable ending. Should we call someone, we wondered. But who would we call? We hadn't had phone signals for hours, hadn't passed anyone else for miles.

WE GOT MARRIED IN A forest clearing, years ago, our friends playing music we danced to. The cake was chocolate and raspberries, vanilla and lingonberry. There were things we agreed on without talking about them. How sour and sweet always had been our favorite combination. How sleeping under the stars was like being on a spaceship, going someplace unknown and far away and somehow still so comfortable. How when we reached out to touch one another, we always kept our pinkies interlocked a second longer than the other fingers.

WE LEFT BEFORE THE BARN fell in, before the aftermath. Inevitability has never been as beautiful as the possibility of something not happening. It might not come to pass. You might never not feel this way. The world might not end. In the car, we hold hands for a second and then drive on. We sing a song we both know the lyrics to. The sound bounces around us. The road is empty. We make noise to fill it, our own happiness an out-of-key duet, in the silence from all sides.

# So Far The Distance

We used to believe that the stars were so bright and far away that they must be gods. Later, we thought that the sky itself might be a great cloth slowly being eaten by moths and the stars were merely light let through from heaven. Once we thought we understood the sky. We said the stars had been dead for years and so we shouldn't care about them anymore. And yet we woke most nights dreaming of them. We chose our star-travelers carefully. We sought them out in places no one had thought to check.

When he was a boy, his mother would tell him to see how far he could leap, and he'd run so fast before he'd let his body leave the earth. His mother, dazzled, clapped her hands at the sight of his body arcing past the sky. She thought he'd be a dancer.

Another was a swimmer. Before she knew the sky, she knew the sea. They were both so endless and deep. Her sister braided her hair into plaits and said, "Go out and be brave." The waves would crash over her and the tide would pull her deep but she never let the water steal her breath.

We told them tales only fit for night, as the stars blinked in and out around us, and in their dreams they thought they could hear someone whispering. And so many of them woke to find themselves afraid. Of how the stars were so far. Of how they might never swim between the darkness and the shining.

When they placed their bodies into capsules, we prayed for them to be safe, to find what they were seeking, even though we had not prayed for years. The stars were not gods, they were too far away for that.

We watched them when we could. Dipped into their dreaming and tried to see what they saw. From inside these metal houses, the sky looked black as the pools of their eyes. We saw no stars.

○

B<small>UT STILL THEY DRIFTED THROUGH</small> the night. They thought of jumping, of water crashing. They thought of home and wondered what their loves were doing so far away from them.

I<small>N YEARS AND YEARS AND</small> years, children will gaze up at the night sky to look for constellations, study the stories told by pinpricks of light. We know that our travelers will still be soaring, but the children will think that those flashes are simply shooting stars.

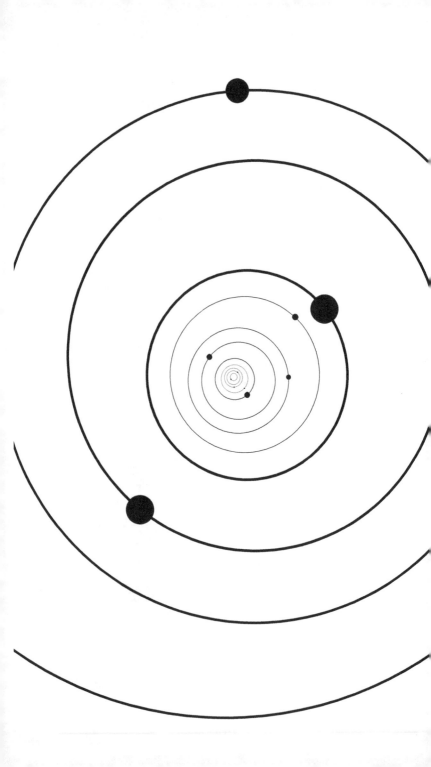

# Acknowledgments

As I was writing these stories, the oldest and most recent nearly fifteen years apart in their earliest drafts, I never thought about the connections between them. However, as I began to form a collection and edit them into a cohesive whole, I realized one of the biggest, my biggest, preoccupations in them is the orbit of people who surround the protagonists. Who do we love and how do they help us? What do we owe to one another and how do we honor those who surround us? In life, we all have our own galaxies. These stories were written in mine and so I'd like to thank those who I am lucky enough to orbit beside.

The editors, staff, and readers of the literary journals where versions of these stories first appeared were elemental in helping me to finetune these pieces. Running a literary magazine is a time-consuming work of dedication and I am thankful that people are willing to do it.

Everyone at Baobab has been amazingly kind, receptive, and brings their excellent critical eyes in a way that always feels productive and caring for the stories themselves. Thank you Danilo, Christine, Margaret, and everyone. I couldn't have asked for a better home for this collection.

Thank you so much to some of my favorite authors, who so graciously agreed to give blurbs: Sequoia Nagamatsu, Ben Loory, and Matt Bell. Please read their books!

With any book there is no way to thank everyone who was a friend, support, etc. But I want to try: Kate Mead-Brewer, Hannah Grieco, Chris Corlew, Ellie Gordon, Crystal Stone, Beth Gilstrap, David Longhorn, Gretchen Rockwell, Amy Barnes, Ellen Rhudy, Lisa Koca, Maria Rago, Peter and Vasti Brown, The Martins Families, JJ and Jayvian Antunes, Sara Doan, Marc "Yoda" Seals, Tara Stillions Whitehead, Addie Tsai, Rita Mookerjee, M. Molly Backes, Zara Chowdhary, Carla Ferreira, Holly Walrath, Jordan Kurella, Vance Kotrla, Courtney Martin and Adam Peck, Kanika Lawton, Jennifer Fliss, Philippe Meister, E. Kristen Anderson, the staffs at my local coffee shops over the fifteen years this was written, and so many more who I am, of course, forgetting.

Stephanie Gunn—for reading everything I write and boldly

encouraging me in my strangest ideas. Matt Paul–for being a terrific long-distance friend and Oreo-compatriot. My co-Xenos in chief: Hannah Cohen and Teo Shannon–for being gleefully bitchy with me about Oreos and being wonderfully amazing when it matters. Erin Schmiel–for many coffee-fueled rants and always being the best. Gillian Ramos–for being endlessly supportive and kind and letting me send way too many memes. Brontë Wieland–for engaging in evil plots, frightening me with hideous food monstrosities, and creating a long-distance best house. My grandmother, Millie Hatch, for being wonderful. My parents have encouraged every bit of story and art I have ever done, and so all of these stories are always for them. My brothers, nephew beasts, and sister-in-law, for much love. And Brian Ramos, for being the best partner in travel, in art, in life.

Stories in *Patterns of Orbit* previously appeared in the following publications:

"There Is the World Within This Window" in *Atlas & Alice*
"A Sense of Taste" in *Anomaly*
"Even the Night Sky Can Learn to Be a Fist" in *Little Fiction*
"The Waves Hear Every Promise You Make" in *Khora*
"A Place You Know" in *Smokelong Quarterly*
"This Skin You Call Your Own" in *X-Ray*
"Swingman" in *monkey bicycle*
"Buoyancy" in *CRAFT*
"Who Walks Beside You" in *Supernatural Tales*
"Simultaneity" in *Wyvern*
"Wearing the Body" in *Louisiana Literature*
"Even the Veins of Leaves" in *Supernatural Tales*
"Run the Line" in *Words & Sports*
"Static" in *Midnight Breakfast*
"Supernova" in *No Contact*
"Jumpers" in *Lady Churchill's Rosebud Wristlet*
"Advance Step" in *Stymie*
"The Ocean Is Not Empty" in *Modern Language Studies*
"We Are Still" in *Empty House*
"So Far The Distance" in *The Bohemyth*

# Orbits

The cover graphic, "PIA17041: Orbits of Potentially Hazardous Asteroids (PHAs)" (NASA/JPL-Caltech. August 2, 2013) shows the orbits of all the known Potentially Hazardous Asteroids (PHAs), numbering over 1,400 as of early 2013. These are the asteroids considered hazardous because they are fairly large (at least 460 feet or 140 meters in size), and because they follow orbits that pass close to the Earth's orbit (within 4.7 million miles or 7.5 million kilometers). But being classified as a PHA does not mean that an asteroid will impact the Earth: None of these PHAs is a worrisome threat over the next hundred years. By continuing to observe and track these asteroids, their orbits can be refined and more precise predictions made of their future close approaches and impact probabilities.

One of the highlighted orbits is that of binary asteroid Didymos around the Sun. Didymos consists of a large, nearly half-mile-wide (780-meter-wide) asteroid orbited by a smaller, 525-foot-wide (160-meter-wide) asteroid, or moonlet. Didymos' smaller asteroid was the target of NASA's Double Asteroid Redirect Test (DART) mission. NASA's DART mission launched to Didymos at 1:21 a.m. EST on Nov. 24, 2021, on a SpaceX Falcon 9 rocket from Vandenberg Air Force Base in California.

DART intercepted the smaller moonlet asteroid at 7:14 p.m. EDT on Sept. 26, 2022. DART impacted Dimorphos at high speed–about 4 miles or 6.6 kilometers per second. Dimorphos was about 6.8 million miles (11 million kilometers) from Earth at the time of DART's impact.

The goal of the mission was to determine how much DART's impact altered the moonlet's velocity in space by measuring the change in its orbit around Didymos.

Prior to DART's impact, it took Dimorphos 11 hours and 55 minutes to orbit Didymos. After DART's intentional collision with Dimorphos on Sept. 26, 2022, astronomers used telescopes on Earth to measure how much that time had changed. The investigation team confirmed the spacecraft's impact altered Dimorphos' orbit around

Didymos by 32 minutes, shortening the 11-hour and 55-minute orbit to 11 hours and 23 minutes. (This measurement has a margin of uncertainty of approximately plus or minus 2 minutes.)

Before its encounter, NASA had defined a minimum successful orbit period change of Dimorphos as a change of 73 seconds or more. The early data showed DART surpassed this minimum benchmark by more than 25 times.

"This result is one important step toward understanding the full effect of DART's impact with its target asteroid," said Lori Glaze, director of NASA's Planetary Science Division at NASA Headquarters in Washington. "As new data come in each day, astronomers will be able to better assess whether, and how, a mission like DART could be used in the future to help protect Earth from a collision with an asteroid if we ever discover one headed our way."

The orbital diagram was produced by the Center for Near Earth Object Studies (CNEOS), which is managed by NASA's Jet Propulsion Laboratory in Southern California. CNEOS characterizes every known near-Earth asteroid (NEA) orbit to improve long-term impact hazard assessments in support of NASA's Planetary Defense Coordination Office (PDCO).

- information summarized from NASA's Jet Propulsion Laboratory website:
*https://www.jpl.nasa.gov/images/pia17041-orbits-of-potentially-hazardous-asteroids-phas*
*https://www.jpl.nasa.gov/images/pia24565-the-orbit-of-asteroid-didymos*

The cover text of *Patterns of Orbit* is set in ⋂ΛSΛLIZΛTIO⋂, an ultramodern sans serif typeface with a nod to the 1975 Nasa logo.

The headers are set in **Adobe Caslon Pro**, William Caslon released his first typefaces in 1722. Caslon's types were based on seventeenth-century Dutch old style designs, which were then used extensively in England. Because of their remarkable practicality, Caslon's designs met with instant success. Caslon's types became popular throughout Europe and the American colonies; printer Benjamin Franklin hardly used any other typeface. The first printings of the American Declaration of Independence and the Constitution were set in Caslon. For her Caslon revival, designer Carol Twombly studied specimen pages printed by William Caslon between 1734 and 1770. The OpenType Pro version merges formerly separate fonts (expert, etc.), and adds both central European language support and several additional ligatures.

The body is set in Cormorant Garamond. Cormorant is an open-source serif family designed by Christian Thalmann. The design was inspired by the sixteenth century types of Claude Garamond, however, in contrast to typical Garamond-inspired text faces, Cormorant was designed as a display face.